*The Storm
in my Mind...*

The Storm in my Mind...

Ami, Kolkata and Confessions

AYAAN BASU

Srishti

PUBLISHERS & DISTRIBUTORS

SRISHTI PUBLISHERS & DISTRIBUTORS
N-16, C. R. Park
New Delhi 110 019
editorial@srishtipublishers.com

First published by
Srishti Publishers & Distributors in 2013

Typeset by EGP

"I couldn't sleep last night because I know that it's over between us. I'm not bitter anymore, because I know that what we had was real. And if in some distant place in the future we see each other in our new lives, I'll smile at you with joy and remember how we spent the summer beneath the trees, learning from each other and growing in love. The best love is the kind that awakens the soul and makes us reach for more, that plants a fire in our hearts and brings peace to our minds, and that's what you've given me. That's what I hope to give to you forever. I love you. I'll be seeing you..."

– THE NOTEBOOK

To

Anushka

&

Kaira

Acknowledgments

No one sails alone on the voyage of life. When the joy of completion arrives, I take this opportunity to thank those who stayed with me, walked beside me, believed in my ability and helped me along in a way that continuously urged me to write this book.

I take immense pleasure in thanking my parents and sister for their inspiration, encouragement and motivation throughout the phase of creating this book.

My friends for being the surrogate family and inspiring me along with my readers, while subconsciously contributing to the content of the book.

And finally, the catalyst, Srishti Publishers and their entire team for the recognition and encouragement.

Sarah for assisting in the editing part to finally reach here. Thanks to her, my writing became more streamlined and thoughts materialized into this concrete beginning for the nostalgic influence of my hometown, Kolkata.

KOLKATA (2007)

1

Graveyard shift and a good friend ...

College exams have been over for a few days now. When someone really gets tied up in books for a while, one tends to forget what it's like to be employed and on the job. It has been a week since I am back to work, catching up with the pace.

All round the week, I had ... Oh so quiet ... Oh so still ... moments around the house till Friday finally arrived.

Friday finally! Today is the last working day of this week. The workplace is bustling with energy as everyone is ready to be emotionally homeless to embrace the happy weekend mood.

I celebrated the addition of new friends from the time I started working, but I also said goodbye to some of them and connected with others who I had not seen in years.

My phone rang, "Bro, where are you?"

"On the way dude, I had a late pick-up today; I should be reaching in another quarter of an hour. Where are you?" I asked.

"Waiting for you at the rear gateway at the chaiwala's shop."

"Okay, will reach and call you."

Hello Everyone: Aryan Roy, age-twenty-two, final year engineering student (Information Technology)- National Institute of Technology, currently working as a Senior Associate in Wipro Info-tech, Salt-lake Sector five for the last two years. Well, how else would I earn bucks for pocket money?

My work life is dictated by these nights.

Luke Kenny fans have termed it 'graveyard shift'. It reminds us of Hollywood horror movies *and working all alive among all living beings*. During the night shift boom in India, several stories linked up to the term graveyard shift. I read one such story in an article about graveyards, written in the early nineteenth century, where the graveyard caretaker continued to rig caskets with bells in case a "corpse" happened to wake up during their shift. The term related to the profession of working at night while the world sleeps is, hence, the graveyard shift.

The funny thing is, when I was told about the graveyard shift working hours, surprise struck me; I was left thinking for long, "Why is it such an unattractive deadly name?" It reminded me of strange supernatural stories. We would often come across first hand stories during my middle school days about the famous graveyard behind the National Library in Kolkata.

I took admission in the Engineering College, but my reduced capacity of adjusting with my fellow mates robbed me of interest in college life. Life was too uncomplicated, undemanding and trouble-free for them: it was always about chatting, gossiping, hanging out and having fun. I, on the other hand wanted to take life seriously, so I decided to work and here I am. Working during the night and sleeping during the day. I managed to grace my presence in a handful of essential lectures with an unfinished sleep for those days. But I enjoyed it!

There were times when my college batchmates, their parents and also my relatives scrutinized me with uncanny expressions since I worked night shifts. Misconceptions about working in night shifts used to be very high during that time. We were thought to be a bunch of dumb people, appraising the enraged international customers. During the initial days, it used to infuriate me, but gradually I got to the point of thinking that it was lack of appropriate exposure to this social change and the new faces of our developing motherland. Maybe someday this mindset and this thinking would gradually lead to acceptance.

Night shifts are supposedly the synonym for a call center, though we all know that it is not necessarily so. Don't get me wrong here – I work for the Hardware support for one of the major American multi-national companies, a primary project in Wipro outsourcing as a contributing team member for the past two years.

Anyway, back to the conversation, at 1.45 a.m., my cab reached the Wipro campus. The shift was at 2.30 a.m.; I had time with me. The rest of the employees had already geared up to set off for the weekend and were waiting at the parking lot for the company cabs to drop them home. I called Faiyaz, "Dude where are you?"

Faiyaz said in his charming voice, "Where are you *matlab*? I am at the same place – back gate, chai ka dukaan."

"Okay will be there in a few minutes. Bye."

"Bye."

I had met Faiyaz during my voice and accent training in Wipro a year back. Those ten days of my voice and accent training are cherished till date. I found my soul friends there and Faiyaz Khan was one of them.

Bald, about 5 feet 8 inches tall with a black framed set of spectacles over his nose, studded ear. He was in Mumbai for the past four years, adorned with his typical Mumbaikar *"tereko, mereko, apun ka"* scattered in his accent.

Two days of ceremonial hi and hello and we became friends, thanks to Gautam sir, our voice and accent trainer who recommended the fifteen-minute breaks during training for our refreshment.

I reached the front gate at 1.45 a.m. The rest of the employees who had just got done with their shift were gearing up to hit off for the weekend.

Faiyaz was at the tea shop at the back gate with a cup of tea in his right hand and a cigarette in his left.

He saw me, smiled and said, "How are you, bhai?"

"Good, *aur tu bataa*?"

"*Mast, jhakkas.*"

I ordered a tea, "Dada, one tea."

The chai wala handed me a cup and on my first sip, I longed for a cigarette. I asked my mate Faiyaz if he had a cigarette with him.

He took out one from the packet. I lit it and started with our regular conversations – daily rituals like office episodes, common friends and many others.

Faiyaz said, "Hey, I heard there's a client call after the shift?"

I was taken aback, "Hell no way, that's crazy … Shit!!"

Curious and surprised, Faiyaz charged me, "What happened? Why shit?"

"Naah! It's nothing really, chuck it."

"*Arre bol na.*"

"Anushka is in town; she was planning to meet me."

"Aha, she is finally here! So, you're planning to catch up, I reckon?"

"Yes."

"So what's the problem? Tomorrow being a Saturday, you could both meet any time of the day, yea?"

"Yes, we could, but she insisted for a movie followed by lunch."

Faiyaz responded furiously, "Dude, you are working all night followed by a client call and a longer day than usual. The client call is important and so are your few hours of rest, post a hectic week. Just lunch is acceptable, but movie before that?"

Too many sensible protests and Faiyaz can never be debated with.

The best way was to keep quiet, which I did. A while later I said, "I told her I would make it; I was unaware about this client call."

Faiyaz retorted harshly, "She came down from Delhi for a vacation, right? The movie would not walk away from the theatre even if you postpone it to Sunday."

"I don't know, let's see."

Faiyaz lit one more cigarette. His reactions weren't new to me.

Angry or irritated, he would use smoking as a stress-buster.

He asked, "*Toh,* what's your plan?"

I passed the cigarette, took a puff and replied, "Nothing much, she wants to watch the 11.45 a.m. show in Priya cinemas and maybe lunch later."

"This movie plan was yours?"

"No, not really; it was hers and I told her that you would also be joining us."

"What?"

"Yes mate, you're one of the few people I talk about mostly to her, so she's really keen on meeting you."

"You and your so-called girlfriend."

Both of us started walking towards our building. The shift was to start in ten minutes.

While on the way back I asked, "Faiyaz, tell me something?"

"*Kya?*"

"You don't like Anushka much, do you?"

He gave a gentle smile and said, "You never gave me the chance to meet her mate, so no comments. I've only heard the good things you said about her. Let's meet her tomorrow, then I should be able to give you an honest feedback."

I laughed and punched his shoulder lightly, *"Nataunki!"*

Faiyaz told me, "Listen, cancel the movie plan. *Waise* your relation with her is no less than a movie, we can meet up just for lunch."

I looked at him for his sarcastic comment and nodded.

We entered our bay as work was soon to commence.

2

The predictable horrible meeting!

The meeting with our clients went well, predictably! Throughout the meeting I did a mind reading of the clients' representative; I gathered that frustration was holding them back and complications strangling them ... strange huh!

On late mornings, the lush green massive campus of Wipro looks amazing. Standing in the smoking zone with Faiyaz, Sufiyan and Indrajeet, we were discussing our day at work over a smoke.

Sufiyan asked me, "So Aryan, *kya plan hai weekend ka*?"

Before I could answer, Faiyaz took over, "He's going for a date; mark my words, it's not a blind date this time," and winked at me.

Indrajeet became curious. He asked, "I'm sorry, I didn't quite get you?"

Faiyaz looked at me and smiling he said, "*Arre* just kidding, bhai is going for a date."

Sufiyan smiled, "All the best, have fun."

Like a polite guy I said, "Thank you".

Faiyaz accompanied me. The plan was to go to my place and do some touch ups here and there and head over to meet Anushka.

It was already 12.30 p.m., so our chance of watching the movie did not click. I don't know how many times I blighted our client for scheduling the congregation that day.

We boarded the 1.00 p.m. cab. I kept my bag inside the car and leaned against the front door of the car. Just then, my mobile rang.

"Hello."

"Idiot, where are you?"

"Hi Anushka."

"Hi."

"I just left my work place, where are you?"

"Since you cancelled the movie plan, I came out for a movie with Kaira. What's your plan?"

"I'm on the way home with Faiyaz. Will go freshen up and maybe catch you later once you're done with the show?"

"Okay."

"By the way, what time is the show?"

"1.45 ... Priya cinema, Deshapriya Park."

"Okay, that means the movie would be over by 3.15 and what about our lunch plans?"

"No worries! We can have lunch at 4 after we all meet. By the way, are you coming with Faiyaz?"

"Sounds good to me. And yes, I am coming with him. Now who is Kaira?"

"Great, why?"

"Is she the ex-school friend of yours from Mumbai?"

"Yes."

"Okay, so she's back in town?"

"Umm, she's on vacation. It's just a short visit here in Kolkata and she'll return to Mumbai by the end of next week."

"Okay."

"Aryan, I've got to hang up now; will ring you up when the movie ends."

"*Thik hai*, send me a text during intermission then will head out from here."

"Okay."

"*Chalo*, bye."

"Bye."

Faiyaz was tuning to the sound of the radio on his cell phone and I fell asleep to it.

3

Flashback (3 years ago)
Entry of the online friend

As we were waiting for the movie to end, I reminisced a little about the life I led three years earlier. That was a time when online friendship was overrated. We would search for friends, introduce each other and nurture the bond. Most of them disappeared into thin air with time. Few stayed and we bonded. I came to know this girl through Yahoo messenger.

I was finishing my high school, preparing for my final exam, concentrating on all the critical classes, making my laboratory work and attending the boring tuitions. There was nothing much to do after tuition classes. I used to set out to a cyber café in the vicinity.

Soon, I discovered the luring world of Yahoo Messenger and Rediff.bol, the anonymous people and those flirtatious chats were high on romantic quotient. Thereafter it was less of a web surfing and more of a girlfriend seeking activity that also honed up my conversation skills. I found nothing wrong in it as it was a part of the teenage craze. Ever since adolescence crept in, I realized that going through hormonal changes could be really confusing.

One evening, after my physics tuition got over, I was exploring different rooms of Yahoo Messenger. I randomly pinged a strange ID, though skeptical about the gender of the account holder. I felt it in me that there was a pretty girl waiting for me at the other end of the monitor.

I got a reply too. ASL (Age, Sex, Location).

I did the same (ASL) and gathered that she's Anushka, final year student – Ballygaunge Siksha Sadan – chatted with her for about ninety minutes, a decent chat session including our hobbies, schools, etc. The best part was we exchanged numbers so that we could continue over the phone.

Although I never really called her at first, she had become a habit. I mean, why would she not be when all we did was chat throughout the day and night. A strange connection with her made me happy to discover that we actually had quite a lot in common.

It took me a month's time to finally decide to call her up and not just stick to chatting. Things tend to get a little too monotonous when you don't think about moving to the next level. Her voice was composed and mature for her age. She was friendly on the chats and nothing seemed changed even over the phone. It felt lonely and weird on days when I didn't hear from her.

One day she requested for a photograph; I was overwhelmed. A girl asking for my photograph? In my head I was like 'Wow! For real?'

We chatted for a month over the telephone. Our conversations would normally last for almost four to five hours. Fortunately, my high school final examination was over two months away, coated with an ample amount of study leave. Each morning my parents would leave for their work by 10 and it was pretty easy for me to call her up and talk to her.

For a normal guy, two months of spending time with a girl over the phone and not seeing each other did not feel normal at all. I had to spice up our conversation a bit in order to get to see her. So this one time I said, "Hey Anushka, would it bother you even for a little bit if I tell you that I'm dying to meet you? Or would it make you happy if I ask if you're least interested in meeting up?" I then giggled to make the situation less awkward.

She laughed for a few seconds and said, "Would you be surprised if I tell you that I've been waiting for you to ask me out?"

I was numb for a second and there was another two-minutes silence of joy and awkwardness between us. I could sense she was equally excited too.

"Why, what's the matter, did I offend you?"

"No, no offense taken." I stammered a little but continued anyway because I did not want to sound like how I was actually feeling from the inside. "Are you sure, Anushka?"

"Ummm.... I'd be lying if I say I wasn't," she giggled sweetly.

"Super!" She actually got me jumping all over.

She kept quiet for a while."What are you doing on Sunday afternoon?"

I took some time to think ... do I have any tuitions ... Yaa lucky me ... No tuitions on Sunday.

I replied, "Well I have some errands to run but I wouldn't mind taking some time out for you."

"That's great. I'll be going to the New Market with my school friends to shop for accessories that day. Would you care to join us?"

I realized that the traditional mindset track of girls still existed. They never meet somebody unfamiliar alone, and she was no different.

I replied, "Okay no issues. What time?"

"How about 2-ish?"

"Sure."

"In front of Citimart, opposite Sreeram Arcade." She paused for a bit and said, "Let's see who wins at hide and seek."

Meeting her finally

Citimart is the all-in-one garment store for budget shoppers in Kolkata just adjacent to the heritage New Market. Earlier it used to be called Sir Stuart Hogg's Market but gradually with time, the name got transformed to New Market, which is some two hundred years old. In spite of being such an old market, it still continues to be the premier shopping centre of Kolkata where you find everything from flowers, cakes, fruits, fishes, junk-foods, movie theater to garments. But the only thing you need to master is the art of bargaining, which is present in the blood of almost every Bengali.

Sunday afternoon finally arrived and I was standing in front of Citimart all alone, too nervous to even look out. From the telephonic conversations we had, I had figured that she liked decent guys.

Not wating to much funky to be precise, I went wearing black denim jeans and a white t-shirt , my favorite attire.

I looked at my watch - five past two and my heart started beating faster – If there's ever a feeling of half completely panicked and half completely freaked out, that's how I felt.

I was looking all around, and every time I noticed groups of young girls, I would ask myself 'would they be them?'

Suddenly I heard a very familiar voice from right behind my back, "Excuse me."

I turned around - a girl in yellow salwar, around 5 feet 5 inches tall, good figure, fair complexion and long hair, looking like a typical beautiful Bengali girl, smiling at me along with three other young girls standing beside her.

I smiled and replied, "yes."

"Aryan?"

"Anushka?"

"Yes, hi."

"Hello." We both shook hands.

"Sorry, I got a little late and kept you waiting."

"Hey, no worries, I'm really glad to see you."

This is what most girls fancy … having a guy wait on her.

I turned towards the three smiling faces standing beside her and said, "They must be your friends?"

"Oh yes, sorry I almost forgot. Meet Parvati, Deblina and Kriti."

All of a sudden, the girl named Parvati, who actually looked like the aunty of the group, asked me, "Hey Aryan, what's your star sign?"

I surprised asked, "Why?"

"Actually Astrology is a passion for me, so I'm just curious."

Proudly, I said, "I'm a Virgo," although I was not convinced with the explanation she gave.

"Okay."

I saw Anushka still smiling at me.

I asked, "What?"

She replied, "Nothing, you look pretty different from that photograph."

"Really! And is the photograph better?"

"Nope, the person standing in front of me is better."

"Aha, thank you."

I noticed each one of them holding one or two paper bags. I looked down at the packet which Anushka was holding and asked, "So, it seems you did some shopping?"

She looked at the packet and then at me, "Yes, just got a pair of jeans and some accessories".

Her friends were busy talking amongst themselves. I tried cracking a few jokes in front of Anushka just to seem a bit jovial. I lowered my voice and asked, "Whenever you go out, do you always carry this bunch of bodyguards along with you?"

She smiled and punched me lightly on my stomach, "Shut up Aryan! They are my angels."

Deblina smiled at me and then looked at her friend, "Hey Anushka, why don't you guys catch up. In the meanwhile we'll take a short trip to Sreeram Arcade to look at some dresses."

She replied, "Okay."

"Alright then, we'll try to be back in another twenty minutes or so."

"Okay."

With all of them smiling at us, they took off.

I was a bit nervous now that we were actually together.

Finally she broke the silence, "So Mr. Aryan, I am standing here in front of you."

"You're absolutely different from what I imagined you'd be like in real life."

"You think so?"

"Yes, seriously."

"Hmm, so how is your preparation for your exams going?"

"Good, pretty boring."

"I know the same condition applies at my end too. How is your rehearsal going on?"

"Good, good. We have a show coming up next month in Santiniketan."

"That's great. I wish I could see you performing."

"Well, if you want you can come along. I don't mind at all."

"Very funny."

Apart from studies and tuitions, I also used to be part of a band named "Driftwood". I was the lead singer and rhythm guitarist for this band. We used to perform whenever we got a chance and practised every weekend. She was aware of this and the good part was she appreciated my talent and interest for music.

I asked her, pointing towards an icecream parlour beside Sreeram Arcade, "Icecream?"

"Sure."

We came to the parlour and ordered a black current cone for me and a chocolate cone for herself.

Girls indeed have a fascination for chocolate.

She bit into her icecream and asked me, "You didn't seem too comfortable with my friends?"

I hesitated a bit, "Nothing as such. I was just taken by surprise when she asked about my starsign."

She laughed for a few seconds and said, "I am sorry about that, Aryan. She has the habit of doing that."

"It's okay, never mind."

"Hey, you told me I'm not like what you imagined me to be in real life, but it's totally the opposite in your case."

"Why so?" I asked.

"You're normally calm and quiet over the phone, so I vaguely pictured you as a very decent guy and see, I was not wrong. By the way, when will I get to see you play the guitar?"

"Well, as I told you, you're always welcome to come to Santiniketan with me."

"I'm not kidding."

"Well, nor am I."

"You know it's not possible. Anyway, what's your plan in the evening?"

"Nothing much, from here I'll head directly towards my rehearsals. What about you?"

"I have Economics tuitions at around 7."

"How boring!"

"I know."

Twenty minutes got over and the time came to meet her bodyguard friends. Both of us came out of the icecream parlour and walked down to the front gate of Sreeram Arcade Mall.

I saw three of her friends standing. Right on time, which actually should not be. I mean, it's a big mall they could have taken some more time exploring all the stores.

Pointing my finger at them, I said, "See, your bodyguards are so punctual."

"Shut up, Aryan!"

I laughed and replied, "Okay, okay."

Parvati asked Anushka as we came near them, "Where did both of you go?"

She replied, "We went to the icecream parlour."

I asked Parvati, "So did you get anything from this mall?"

"Nope, the collection is not that great and a bit overpriced. Anyway we got enough for today,"she showed the packets in her hand.

"Okay."

An awkward silence followed. Suddenly, Anushka caught my left hand and said, "Well Aryan, gotta go now."

I was numb for a few seconds as I stared at her, trying hard to feel the sensation of her hand. Again she repeated, "Aryan!"

I came back to the real world. Quickly I replied, "Oh, but when do we meet again?"

She smiled and replied, "Let's see. Pretty soon, I guess. Call me after you return home."

"I might be late."

"No issues. Call me at your leisure."

"Okay."

Three of her friends bid me goodbye and so did I. I noticed one thing. During my short encounter with them, one of Anushka's friends Kirti didn't utter a word at all. She's probably the quiet kind.

I started walking towards the Esplanade Metro station to catch the metro for Tollygaunge – the place where I practice with my band "Driftwood."

As it was a Sunday, the roadside near the Oberoi hotel was crowded, especially with couples. I was very happy and felt like "Wow, what a girl!" Just like the one I was looking for.

I was also very impressed with her simplicity. She came to meet me just the way she was. I felt like a winner.

Melanche

Sunday night was awe-inspiring for me. I came home, spent some time with Anushka over the phone yet again. All in all, it was a good day and I guess it's safe to say, it was one of those best nights plus a good sleep that I hadn't got in a long long time.

It was like heaven.

The next few days were all bizarre, all tied up with school work, tuitions and all that, but I made it clear to myself that I would at least call her up once every day.

There was this one time when we just couldn't stop... We just couldn't; we went on and on for eight long hours.

As days passed by, I started to feel the confusion running through my mind – 'Are we just really good friends, or are we falling for each other more like an infatuation? Or is it just one sided?'

Most of my school friends are "in love," puppy love of course. We're all too young to be taking things seriouly.

One evening I was at home alone when the telephone rang.

I picked up and said, "Hello."

"Hi."

"Hey Anushka, what's up?"

"What's going on?"

"Nothing, was just watching television but you had your economics tuition in the evening, right?"

"Yes I did, my tutor is not well so she rescheduled our class for next week. I came back home and thought of calling you."

"Why so?"

"Didn't get you Aryan?"

"Nope, nothing."

"Hey Aryan, can I ask you something?"

"Since when did you start taking permission?"

"Shut up! I am serious." Her voice was pretty rude this time.

"Okay, go ahead."

"For the past few days I have noticied that whenever you talk to me you are lost somewhere. I mean you are talking to me but actually you are thinking something else."

I was a bit surprised, "Really?"

"Yes, is everything alright?"

"Yeah, everything is fine. Maybe I am studying hard these days, don't know."

She was not convinced, "I don't think so. Anyway I wanted to tell you something."

"Sure."

"We have our annual school fest *Melanche* this Saturday and I want you to come."

"Nope, not again."

"What, not again?"Surprised she asked me.

"Not again; as in face to face with your bodyguards."

"Please don't start off again. And by the way, they're not my bodyguards; they are my friends."

"Okay, okay, sorry. But you will be tied up with your friends."

Now, in a commanding voice, she asked, "Will you come for me or not?"

This was a direct sentimental attack in which she is a champion. I had no other option. Like a good boy I agreed, "Okay, I will come."

She smiled and said, "That's like a good boy. I will arrange for your pass."

I reached Rashbehari Avenue changing two autos. It was seven in the evening and shame on the heavy traffic.

Thought of calling Anushka and informing her that I would be a little late. Considering the traffic jam, I would take at least thirty more minutes to reach.

I looked for a public booth, then changed my mind.

I could just see her angry face upon my telling her that I'd be late by half an hour, so it was best for me not to call her.

Took another fifteen minutes and I managed to reach near her school. Went to a PCO booth and dialled her cell number. Today I realized the importance of keeping a cell phone.

"Hi."

There was already too much commotion in school where she was. She yelled, "Idiot, where are you?"

"In front of your school."

"Give me two minutes; I am coming outside the main gate."

"Okay."

I almost ran towards the main gate of Ballygaunge Siksha Sadan.

She was already there and my eyeballs got fixed on her.

She looked amazing. Wow – Tight denim jeans, black sleeveless top, long open hair which highlighted her sex appeal.

The simplicity of her dress and the way her hair swayed while she was walking towards me got me all excited.

"Aryan, she is too good," I told myself.

I went near her, she smiled and showed the watch on her wrist, "Mr. Aryan Roy, you are so punctual!" she said sarcastically.

I answered with a smile, "Traffic dear, couldn't help it."

She came a bit closer to me, so close that I could smell her perfume.

"Traffic, oh okay. And I'm now reminded about a certain someone telling me how punctual he is over the phone yesterday."

"*Thik hai.* Now you don't have to stretch that."

The response was pretty straightforward, "*Chalen andar?*"

I obediently followed her.

Nothing special was going on in this fest. Wherever your eyes rolled, you could see food stalls standing still. A huge stage had been put up where some local band were playing "Bryan Adams – Summer of 69."

How can I forget girls? The girls were all around and there were varieties. Girls in all party dresses, mostly highly westernized outfits.

Must say my city Kolkata is changing and the changes are drastic!

This is a big advantage when you come to attend an all girls, school fest … like I mentioned earlier you would definitely find varieties.

I witnessed many couples holding each other around their hips. It looked pretty abnormal to me. Will somebody get lost in this small fest if you don't hold anyone in such a manner?

The two of us were walking to the left of the stage where that band was performing. Now their track had changed to "Metallica – Nothing else matters."

She pointed towards the cold drinks stall and asked me, "You want to have something?"

"No, I'm good, thanks."

"Hmm, okay."

She then shouted at a group standing to the left of the stage calling out a girl's name "Sujata!".

I said, "Thank god!"

"What happened?"

"Didn't notice your bodyguards were around," I said laughing.

"Shut up and come with me."

Wow, that was pretty rude.

I saw two girls walking towards us. The other day she had asked what my star sign was. You never know what she might ask me today.

The two girls stood in front of Anushka – one of them pretty short, around five feet tall but very pretty and dressed decently, wearing a full sleeve white top with black jeans asked her, "Hey, where did you go?"

Anushka replied, "Aryan didn't have the pass so we went outside for his entry pass."

I smiled and raised my right hand toward the short girl, "Hi."

She shook hands and smiled, "Hello Aryan, I'm Sujata. Nice to see you. Have heard a lot about you from your friend."

Looking at Anushka, I smiled and replied, "Oh did she? I wouldn't have really expected that of her. I hope it's all good things though."

"Yeah, she has nothing bad to talk about you, really."

"Really! Good to know."

"Hi, Aryan."

I had totally forgotten there was a girl standing beside Sujata.

Pretty good looking, very fair and the best part was her height, around five feet nine inches. She did not look like a Bengali girl, could be a Marwari or Punjabi, wearing a long denim skirt and a black sleeveless top. All in all, I was impressed by her height; very rare in a city like Kolkata.

I looked at her and forwarded my right hand again like I did before, "Hi, I'm Aryan."

She smiled and shook hands, "Kaira. Nice meeting you, Aryan."

I smiled.

Anushka caught my left hand and said, "Come on, let's take a walk."

"Sure."

Kaira attempted a joke, "Hey Anushka, take a walk but don't do anything mischievous behind the stage."

Before she could say anything, I came to her rescue, "Don't worry Kaira, you can at least trust me on that."

She gave me a stare. Boy, her eyes were awesomely seductive. Every time our eyes met, it was almost like as if she was passing on a message.

Anushka and I went towards a food counter. I said, "Hey, I think Kaira is much better than those groups of bodyguards."

She responded in an irritated voice, "Don't dare to call my girlfriends bodyguards again."

"Okay, relax Miss. I was just joking."

"Hmm ... want to eat something?"

"Anything."

"What do you mean by anything, there must be something specific. Where have you disappeared mentally?"

I had no idea what I was thinking, so I covered up saying, "*Kuch bhi to nahi.*"

"Doesn't seem like it. So, what do you want to eat?"

"How about *puchkas*?"

"Sure, why not!"

This is the one reason that makes me hold my head up high. Whenever there's a talk on Kolkata, each and every food item you taste is just brilliant and there are so many varieties of food that one could experiment with and give your tongue a chance to taste such excellent delicacies.

Whilst gulping down panipuri one after the other, I said, "Hey, your friend Kaira has a really good height."

"I know, in fact she is one of the tallest girls in our school."

"I thought so."

"What?"

"That she's one of the tallest girls in your school."

"*Kya baat hai*, you're very curious about her."

"Nothing of that sort. Just that she doesn't look like she's from here," I continued.

"See? Again! By the way, she is not a Bengali and not your type."

I got a bit curious about her last statement, "Not my type?"

"Oh let's just leave the case; can we talk about something else?"

I still did not give up; I could sense her jealousy.

"Okay dear, for a fact I know no one can be a better match for me than Miss Anushka Banerjee."

"Aacha! Look who's trying to flirt with me now."

"Why, can't I?"

"You are too sweet to do that," she smiled.

"Really?"

"Good that I told you."

There were times when she would make me feel like I could just cuddle, caress and treat her like my very own but as the saying goes "A girl's heart is the biggest mystery in this whole universe," and I think I cannot find a better example other than her.

Melanche fest was nothing special apart from Anushka and a few more hot chicks that made my eyes drool.

I looked at my watch, 9.45 p.m. – pretty late. Time waits for none; I hadn't noticed it at all.

We came out from the school gate to the Ballygaunge main road; Sujata and Kaira accompanied us since they lived not too far from Anushka's house.

We started walking towards Gariahat crossing. The Pantaloons Showroom was still open with plenty of people shopping.

We all were walking. Sujata asked me, "So Aryan, how was the fest, did you like it?"

"Well yeah … it was good. I enjoyed it!"

Another voice came in between, "Should be good, after all he was with Anushka"

I looked at Kaira and said, "Excuse me."

Kaira replied with an attitude, "Yes?"

Sujata and Kaira were walking together and behind them Anushka and I. Hearing that "Yes" from Kaira, I walked past Anushka and reached right beside Kaira. She looked at me.

"So, you were saying something?"

"Yes, I said you must have enjoyed. After all, someone special was there with you."

"What's that suppose to mean?"

"Whatever you assume, sir," she smiled. "Now come on! I was just joking … your friend told me you have a great sense of humour so I was basically just checking ... Chill!"

"Positive?"

"Of course, I am."

"Okay."

I didn't notice Anushka and Sujata watching both of us in surprise.

Anushka asked, "How will you go home?"

"Well, I will go to Jadavpur 8B bus stop with you and from there I will take the S-31 bus."

"Okay." She looked at Kaira, "Kaira you can come with us anyway you have to get down on the way at Dhakuria."

Kaira replied, "Okay."

I asked, "Hey and what about Sujata?"

Sujata replied, "You guys would be going straight from Golpark, while I have to take a right from there so I would be taking an auto from Gariahat crossing."

"Okay."

It was 10 o'clock and Gariahat was still a bustling place. Most of the shops were open and some on the verge of closing down for the day, the hawkers still shouting at their peak voice to sell their products and people still waiting for buses to return home after hours of work for the whole day.

All in all Gariahat is Jomjomat!!! (Rocking) with its bong charms, as always.

Sujata took an auto rickshaw for Golpark and the rest of us for Jadavpur.

There was still a long queue at the auto rickshaw stand. People were eager to go back home after work. There was no other option for us; we stood in the queue.

Sujata was lucky that she got an auto rickshaw in five to seven minutes.

I looked at my watch – 10.23 p.m. I figured I was going to get murdered by my own parents once I reach home. I had told them that I would be back home by 9.30 p.m. Thank goodness for not keeping cell phones back then lest they would have busted me out over the phone itself.

After waiting for fifteen more minutes, we managed to get an auto rickshaw.

Anushka got in first, I in the middle and then Kaira since she would be the first to get off. The traffic wasn't all that tight as it was 10.40 and by god if we did not not reach Jadavpur 8B bus stop before 11 p.m., I could miss the last bus. But I was lucky.

The auto rickshaw was moving at its own speed and there was silence amongst the three of us.

Finally I broke the silence. I asked Kaira "So Kaira, Anushka was telling me you are actually not from Kolkata, is it right?"

She replied, "Yes, my parents are in Mumbai. I just came here to complete my high school"

"Okay, so you would be going back I guess after the final exams?"

"Yes."

We reached Dhakuria. The auto stopped right opposite the Dakshinapan Shopping Complex.

Kaira got down. She turned around and said, "Bye Anushka, will talk to you over the phone," and looking toward me she smiled, "Bye, Aryan. It was nice meeting you."

I replied generously, "Same here, take care."

We reached the front gate of Jadavpur University.

Anushka asked, "So how was your evening?"

I replied, "You were there so no question of the evening being bad, but one thing is there..."

"What?"

"Your friend Kaira has a lot of attitude, but Sujata was sweet."

We finally reached Jadavpur 8B bus depot and I saw S-31 my last bus to reach home waiting. It was a sign of relief for me.

Both of us crossed the road.

She was not able to finish her conversation as we had to get down, but finally she did, "You know Aryan, Sujata is actually a sweet girl and so is Kaira. Just that she was born and brought up in Mumbai. So her mindset, culture is entirely different; initially even I felt the same way as you are feeling, but then I discovered that she is actually a very good person to be with.

"Oh, I see, maybe time will tell."

"I know."

I don't know what made me say to her, "Hey, I wanted to tell you something."

"Yes?"

I didn't know how I should say it and in the meanwhile I could see the S-31 bus coming out of the depot.

"Go Aryan, will talk about this later!"

She was right, I couldn't delay any longer.

She shouted from outside, "Give me a call once you reach home."

I nodded my head as the bus sped off.

Now I was left thinking how my parents would react to my late home-coming; nothing else mattered.

4

My heart finally spoke out...

It had been raining all afternoon. I looked at my watch – 5.30 p.m. – which meant it was almost time for my tuitions. Too lethargic to be going anywhere, I felt the need to just relax and speak to Anushka.

While my mind was pacing back and forth, I could hear my Mom calling me from the kitchen asking me to get ready. I was left with no choice.

I replied, "Yes mom, getting ready in ten minutes."

Suddenly at the back of my head I could hear a voice that said 'bunk the tuition just for today and call her up. No big deal on missing just a single class.'

Ready like a good boy, I stepped out of my house, with heaps of books in my bag.

I boarded an auto from my place, "Behala Chowrasta, *dada.*"

So I settled with moving towards the same phone booth, the spot where I normally spent time with Anushka. Moreover, I had like 110 bucks in my pocket, so I didn't have to worry much.

"Hello," she answered after four-five rings.

"Hi, what's up?"

"Aryan, you're calling me at this odd time. Is everything alright?" It's not like she didn't already know that I had my tuitions at that point of time, but oh well, Surprise, Surprise!

"Technically yes, but my tutor cancelled our class so…" I lied when I could have easily told her the truth.

But when you think about it, she's just not the kind of friend who would understand 'yeah I wanted to talk to you rather than attending tuition'. If only she knew I did it just because I wanted to spend time with her; plus yes, my lethargy.

"And so you thought of calling me?"

"Exactly!"

I smiled, "See, we two are perfect for each other; you read my mind so well."

She smiled back and replied, "Yeah yeah, and anything else?"

"Nope."

We chatted for almost an hour. Running out of topics to talk about never really occurred to us, which made me really happy from within.

So she came up with something which I never really expected of her; and never really wanted the conversation to end like it did.

"Hey Aryan, you were supposed to tell me something?"

"Oh, was I?"

"Yes, before you boarded the bus you told me you wanted to tell me something."

"Oh Ok, yes," I recollected what I was supposed to say that day.

"No, it was just something random," I lied.

She took a deep breath and said, "Aryan, when you know you cannot lie, don't even try."

"Chuck it na Anushka! It's not that important; we can talk about it some other time."

She became more adamant, "No tell me now. I am sure, you have something to tell me."

She had that magic in her voice which always compels me to do things for her own liking. The same thing happened.

I seriously didn't know how to tell her and where to start.

I spoke thus, "Okay, I will tell you but you have to promise me something before that."

"Like what?" she asked curiously.

"You have to promise me that after listening to what I say now, it should not affect our friendship."

"What is it that's making you say that?"

"You got to promise me first, otherwise I shall not utter a word."

I managed to convince her with the promise and then there were a few seconds of silence.

She asked, "Come on tell me ... What are you waiting for?"

I smiled, "No, actually I don't know from where to start."

"Just start from anywhere, will you?" she cribbed.

I took a deep breath.

"Okay, tell me something Anushka, how long have we known each other?"

"Around three months, I guess."

"I know it hasn't been that long to know a person like that, but what am I like to you, really?"

"Why are you asking questions? I thought you wanted to tell me something."

"It's related, so please answer me."

"Okay *baba* ... At first I had the impression that you'd be like the rest of the boys who're just being random on social networks but by now I've started to doubt my assumptions.

"Elaborate please."

"The thing that makes you different from the rest of the guys is that you didn't ask for my number right from the get-go like most of them would; you give me space but at the same time you kept a check even through random chats. That's kind of impressive. It was only when I insisted on giving you my number that we actually started with our phone chats." She stopped for a few seconds and took a breath, "When I started talking to you, I noticed a decency and innocence in your voice."

I interrupted "Innocence?"

"Shut up and let me finish…"

"Oops sorry, carry on."

"Yes, I admire your talents, I think what you do and what you like to do is interesting. You're a down to earth sort of a person and you make me feel like you care for me."

She stopped abruptly.

I got a bit impatient, "What happened?"

She smiled, "And the best thing I like about you is that you are a good listener. You know my needs and you make sure that I actually get to say what I want to."

"So what is so special about that?"

"Maybe it isn't all that special to you, but it is for the other person. You do make me feel special and important."

She stopped.

"Okay."

The word 'okay' made her furious, "What Okay? Now you have your answer, where's mine?"

My voice got a bit shaky and I could literally hear my heart beat, "Look Anushka, I don't know how you're going to stomach this but … Do you remember a couple of days ago at your school, you asked me why I was missing mentally?"

"Yes."

"I tried a lot to figure out the answer and finally realized that I have started liking you."

"Aaww, I like you too Aryan. You're probably one of the best human beings I know."

"Thank you for telling me that, but to be more specific, I love you Anushka and I'm not joking."

Suddenly silence overshadowed both ends of the telephone line as I tried re-collecting what I had said. I had blurted it out without thinking. Oh god! I could still feel my heart beating like a drum.

Silence was broken by a very pleasant and calm voice, "Are you serious, Aryan?"

"Yes, I am. I've been asking myself a lot of times if this friendship was meant to last. I always wished it lasts, 'cause you're someone more special than just a friend. One could share so many secrets with a friend and many of my friends whom I know are in a relationship, they sometimes talk about stuff they're not suppose to..." I stopped for a few seconds. There was no voice from the other end of the phone ... "Hello!"

"Go ahead, I am listening Aryan."

"Many of my mates enjoy talking about the raunchy experiences they've had had with their girl or maybe girl-'friends' and when I pictured you being one of those girls, it wasn't easy. I didn't succeed ... but that's not my point. You see, you're the only person with whom I can talk for hours and talk about so many nothings. And all of these things have compelled me to think that it's not a crush; it's love."

"Aryan, you realized so many things and didn't even care to let me know."

"I'm sorry, I've been meaning to confess ever since your school fest, but I have not been able to until now."

"Aryan, I get where you're saying, but can you tell me for how many times we have met?"

"Twice."

"Then how can you come to such a conclusion?"

"Anushka, it is not necessary to meet often to fall in love. It just happened; I can't control my feelings like that."

Silence again. She then said, "I am nine months elder to you."

"How does it matter?"

"Come on now, one always looks for a man who's mature and elder to you so that the stability in the relationship is sustained. School love stories are very rare."

"So can't we both fall in that rare category?"

"It's not about which category you fall in, it's ... Alright listen, I haven't told you this…"

I asked in a surprised tone, "What?"

"His name is Rupam – a software engineer working in Infosys, Bangalore."

"So?"

She went on, "He is four years elder to me and we've been dating for the past one year. My family also likes him."

"And what about you … do you love him?"

"I don't know about love, but yes I fancy him a lot. He's a good person: he is educated, settled, working for a big multinational company. I mean every girl like me wishes and wants her man to be like that."

I was totally numb and didn't know what to say.

"Aryan, are you there?"

"Yes, I am listening."

She went on in a soft and calm voice, "Look Aryan … listen to me, I apologize for not bringing this up earlier when I should have. For now I reckon you should give some time to your career and maybe grow eventually. I'm not saying that you're immature or anything, you get my point right?"

"Can't you wait for me?"

She made her best efforts to convince me, "Look … I mean, I like Rupam and you're a really good friend of mine … please dear, try to understand."

"It's okay, you might not live to wait for me, but I can."

"Come on Aryan, now don't act like a kid. It is time for you to study, not to think about love and all."

"You know Anushka, I always thought there are no conditions in love, but today you gave me a total different definition about love."

"Go home Aryan, I will talk to you later. You reach home then we will talk."

I kept quiet.

She spoke, "Be practical, there are a few things which you need to consider before you can seriously commit and I don't think I have done or said anything wrong."

"Alright Anushka, *chalo* I'm going home. I will talk to you later."

"Are you okay?"

"Oh yes, I do not worry. I will talk to you later. Bye."

"Bye, take care."

I didn't even respond to what she said at the end of the conversation and disconnected the call.

When you tell someone you love them and in return they tell you they love another, it feels like you just got stabbed over and over again.

5

REJECTED AND DEJECTED

That particular day was just crazy, throughout the day I thought about Anushka. I dreamt of so many things but in the end nothing really turned out to be positive.

She used to see me just as a good friend and even cared for me but all the while she's been seeing someone else and never cared to tell me. I was only a little boy who cared much about a girl, but immature enough not to make her love me back.

I knew Anushka would call me and she did too, but I never responded to her calls.

I felt guilty that I had made her a promise that day, and now I was the one who was spoiling our friendship.

Those were tough days for me. I literally fought to concentrate on my studies; high school final exams were just two weeks away. My rehearsals over the weekend also came to a halt because of my exams.

Preparation for the exam was alright but my real fear was Mathematics, as I always thought of that subject as a "Yamraaj".

It was a week to go for the exams. I went to cyber café two days back and saw an offline message from Anushka. "*Hi Aryan, this is not fair yaar, you told me to promise something that day over the phone and I kept my promise. So now what's your problem? I called you so many times and you didn't even cared to call back ... Anyway hope things are fine at your end ... Take care and all the very best for your exams."*

Shall I call her? I asked myself reading the offline message?

I got confused and then decided to call her up at least to wish her all the best.

I waited for my parents to go for work- checked my watch 10.30 – dialed her number.

"Hi Anushka."

"Hi Aryan! so you got my message?"

"Yes, just called in to wish you all the best for your exams."

"Hmm and…?" she smiled.

"And nothing, I would be busy studying so thought of just wishing you."

"Dear, even I am taking exam along with you, so please don't give me that reason."

"I think I should keep the phone down now ... take care."

"Now, listen to me first!"

"What?"

"What's wrong with you, Aryan?" she asked in a loud voice.

I nearly lost my sense listening to this, "You are asking me, what's wrong with me ... you?"

"Yes, I have called you for over a week but you never cared to respond."

"Don't call me ... do one thing, call up your so-called boyfriend and chat with him. Infosys guy, after all."

She paused for a few seconds and then pounced on me, "Listen Aryan, you don't have the right to command me to do anything like that or say anything about my relationship with him."

I completely lost my senses, "Excuse me, what do you mean?"

"You are no one to whom I have to give explanations, just go to hell!"

I was shattered with that last statement -"*Just go to hell!*"

I shouted at her, "Miss Anushka Banerjee, you got a guy and this is the way you talk to a friend. I am ashamed that I know someone like you. Shit, you are such a waste ... you judge love with success and career. Just fuck off!"

There was complete silence on both ends of the telephone line.

She spoke, "Okay and listen Aryan, don't even dare to call me ... I don't want to recall ever that I knew a guy like you. Create an identity of yours before pointing your finger at others."

I did not reply; my hand was trembling. Just banged the phone down.

I remember that night. Skipped dinner. Just cried the whole night. It's unbelievable the way the girl I admired so much got back at me.

I felt guilty at having reacted in such a manner. Thought of calling her up to apologize but just one sentence from her prevented me from doing so, "*Create an identity of yours before pointing your finger at others.*"

I tried my level best to keep all these things apart and concentrate on my studies. Just three days and my high school exams woud start.

Love is really a strange creation of hormonal release within our body. It makes you the lead actor of a romantic play on the stage without a script and proper rehearsal. One can refer to thousands of viewers watching you. If your acting has power, it is directly proportional to a successful love story; and if acting is weak, then romantically you will be molested numerous times in a conscious and sub-conscious state of mind.

I remember how I took the exams. Whenever I was writing the answers sitting in the exam hall, just one sentence was echoing in my ears, "Create an identity of yours before pointing your finger at others."

6

High school exams over; time for a career choice

Exams got over and never had I the chance to even take a break because it was followed by a much bigger exam. I finally had to choose my career.

I always wanted to study mass communication and make my identity as a successful journalist but the same sentence from Anushka "Create an identity for yourself before pointing fingers at others" came back to me time and again.

I made up my mind; I will appear for all the engineering entrance examinations and show her what I was capable of. Engineering clearly meant mathematics and it's still "*yamraaj*" for me but I was adamant.

There was one particular quote that helped me to move ahead with this decision: "*People often say that motivation doesn't last. Well, neither does bathing ... that's the reason we recommend it.*"

My parents were very happy with my decision as my dad and elder sister are also engineers. They always had the expectation from me to follow in their footsteps.

In total, I appeared for four entrance examinations and finally it clicked with our West Bengal joint examination where I managed to secure a decent rank to qualify for Computer Science Engineering.

I was too excited for my entrance exam result to be out.

After waiting for four long weeks, the result was out. I did not score a very good percentage, but enough to fall under the eligibility criteria for Computer Science and Engineering.

My parents were really happy with my initial success but they never knew how I made it and why I made it.

Anyway I thought of calling up Anushka once just to give her the good news. After a lot of hesitation, I dialled her number.

Her mom picked up the phone, "Hello."

"Hello aunty, can I talk to Anushka?"

Banglish (Bengali + English tone) continued from the other end of the phone line.

"Who is speaking?"

"This is Aryan, aunty."

"Oh Aryan, she is not in Kolkata anymore. She's now in Delhi...And how was your result?"

"I scored 72% and got selected from computer science engineering. Has she gone for a vacation?"

"No, didn't she tell you? She shifted to Delhi last week for Law admission."

"What?" I was taken by surprise.

There was no response from my end; I didn't know what to say?

"Hello ... Hello ... Aryan, are you there?"

It took some time for me to come back from that recent shocking news, "Yes aunty."

"Congratulations beta, and all the best for your future."

"Thank you aunty. When you get to speak with Anushka please inform her that my results are out."

"Sure."

'Take care, bye."

"Bye." She kept the phone down.

I sat beside my phone for almost thirty minutes; I didn't know how to react. She shifted to Delhi and didn't even inform me. And above that, not even a call to know my results.

I proposed to her and she rejected, that was fine; but being a good friend she could have at least called up to know my results. These are actually small little things, which hurt you more in life than bigger ones.

It's always possible for me to sit on the mountain top without any pain, but if someone says I should sit on top of a needle, it really hurts!

Engineering – a new world!

My parents were very happy on the first day of my college. I too was excited, but seeing those fat books of Mechanics /Electronics and thinking "my god now I have to study these fat books for four years ... four long years" always made me feel jittery.

College was great but regrettably there was a big communication gap between most of my college mates and me.

I had done my entire schooling from an English medium Catholic School and most of my friends were from Bengali medium, so most of the time we had differences.

They were good, friendly and helpful, but somehow I was not able to adjust.

Two years passed ... learnt a lot from computer languages to electronics, but my interest was more in database applications and networking technologies.

My Didi suggested that I should get some part time job to improve my skills and that's where Wipro came into the picture. I never thought I would get selected there at one go in a project of a leading multinational hardware organization where I could strengthen my hardware and networking skills.

Initially, it was a difficult time for me, working in night shifts and attending only some important lectures in college during daytime. But after three to four months of hardship, I managed to adjust myself and started loving my job. I successfully completed one-and-a-half years with this organization. Additional package: made some very good friends among whom Faiyaz Khan's name tops the list – who always has stood by me in good and bad times.

Suddenly life became so eventful for me with a mix and match of studies, work and friends, that boredom never dared to intrude.

Working and studying hard throughout the week and then partying hard the whole weekend with Faiyaz and the gang. As we used to work in night shift, on weekends we would always go out after 8 p.m. and then the whole night out of the house. How could I forget *Balwant Singh's Chai ka Dhaba*?

One of the shops in Kolkata, which remains open the whole night. They serve Kesar flavoured tea in matti ka *cup, which adds a fabulous taste and when its 4.00 a.m. in our watch,* kachori *and* samosa *normally took care of our weekend breakfast.*

Surprise, Surprise!

I clearly remember that Saturday evening. I was out with Faiyaz and the gang to watch a late night movie. It was just ten minutes after the intermission when my phone rang. I looked at the number which flashed up on the screen. Unknown number with some different STD code.

I rushed out of the hall to the lobby, my phone was still ringing. I received the call.

"Hello."

"Hi Aryan, how are you?" It was a female voice.

"I am doing good, thank you, but I am sorry I can't recollect your voice." I apologized generously.

"Stupid, you forgot my voice. This is Anushka"

I froze for a few seconds. I was thinking, "What the F ***?"

"Aryan, are you there?"

I replied "Hey Anushka, what a pleasant surprise! How are you?"

"I am doing well"

"By the way, who gave you my number?"

"Simple, I searched on Orkut, found you there, went through your profile and luckily got your number."

"Pretty smart, where are you now?"

"Delhi."

We were both quiet for some time. I was still not believing that she called me nearly after two years. There was complete blackout for a few seconds from both ends.

She spoke, "So how's life?"

"Good, in fact, great! Hey, can I call you back later? I'm out watching a movie with my friends."

"Sure, call me whenever you feel like, enjoy your movie. Chalo bye, take care."

"You take care, bye."

I was speechless. I went to the washroom and looked at myself in the mirror. I was talking to the mirror. "Why would she call me?"

Maybe she misses me, or maybe she's back in my life for round two. I in fact, there could be loads of reasons. Without thinking further, I just washed my face and went back to my seat, having missed almost twenty minutes of the movie.

Tried a lot but somehow my mind was getting diverted somewhere else. "*Why did she call me after such a long time?*"

The movie was a total waste for me. I was not able to concentrate, every time her face flashed in front of my eyes. Why would someone put a dagger in your heart and then come to see if you're ok or not after ages?

Faiyaz was a bit curious. He realized something was wrong with me, as I was not behaving the way I normally do.

He asked me after the movie, "What happened, who called you?"

I avoided the topic by saying mom had called up with some minor issues at home.

I tried to console myself saying, "It's ok dear, call her and find out the reason why she called you all of a sudden. At least it won't bother you then."

It was difficult for me the next day, talking to the overseas customers over the phone. A few were disappointed as they expected a resolution from me, calling all the way from the United States.

I walked up to my manager and asked for one-hour break.

He asked me, "Are you okay Aryan?"

"Yes Aniket, I am just not able to concentrate. Need a break, not feeling well," I took a deep breath.

He gave me a stare, "Is everything alright?"

I hesitated, "Yeah, I mean no, Aniket. I am a bit disturbed; some personal issues."

"Oh, do you want to go home?"

"Oh no, not home. If you could give me two hours break, I'll just get my mind freshened up."

Aniket looked at his desktop and thought over something.

He looked at me, "Okay, go ahead. But are you sure you will be fine in two hours?"

"Oh yes, I will, thank you so much," I smiled at him.

He replied with a smile, "No problem."

I tried to spot the cubicle where Faiyaz was sitting. He was late for work that day. I traced him out but he was taking a call, so didn't bother to disturb him. I thought of going to the tea shop opposite the main gate and send him a text message.

I came out of the main gate. This is what I love about Wipro. When you come outside the campus, you will see a huge parking area with hundreds of cars leaving every minute, full light across the entire area, a few of the hawkers have set up their own small business at midnight making some tea shops but not only limited to tea. I think the menu included bread with a combination of butter or egg, wide varieties of biscuits, tea and how can I forget, almost all brands of cigarettes. The funniest part being that you rarely get to see people eating, but if one did not see a person smoking, it was not normal.

It was 3.30 a.m. but the entire place looked like late evening.

I took a cup of tea and a cigarette and found a quiet and silent place to sit a little far off from the crowd which had gathered near the small tea shop.

I thought of sending a text to Faiyaz, but unknowingly landed up in the contact list. The name I searched was "Anushka". I had saved her Delhi number when she had called up the other evening.

It was quarter to 4 and I was thinking of calling her up, knowing well that everyone's not a bat like me. I settled down thinking that she must be sound asleep, but I dialled her number anyway.

There was no response.

I re-dialled her number.

Eight rings later, there was a response, "Hello," said a half sleepy tone.

"Hello Anushka."

Sleepy tone continues, "Hello ... who's this?"

"Aryan here."

A few seconds of silence followed. This time the tone changed, a little less than half sleepy, "Aryan, you're calling up so early in the morning; is everything alright?"

"Yeah yeah I am ok; I am sorry I called up so late."

"Don't be..."

I took a puff from my cigarette, "I was thinking of calling you up in the afternoon, but was a bit tied up."

"No problem, you don't have to give me explanations. It's okay"

Few seconds of silence again.

"So Aryan, you work for a call center? I saw in your Orkut profile."

"Not a call center...I work for hardware consumer support."

"Okay okay, don't be annoyed. I am sorry, we mostly think the people who work at night are employed in a call centre."

"Well, in that case I am afraid to inform you that it's not right."

She smiled, "You know something; you have changed a lot."

"Have I?"

"Yes, you have. Why all of sudden these night shifts and all? You are doing your engineering, right?"

"Yes I am, I mean just attending the important classes and working here, but now I have adapted myself to it."

"But why? After your degree, you will get a job, you know."

"Well, it's a long story; will narrate some other time. How is your college going on?"

"Good, in fact very good. But only one bad thing"

"What?"

"It's going to take five years for me to complete this Law course and that's too far away."

"Ah! Come on, you're basically done with half of five years; you'll be done with it in no time."

"I know, but still..."

We chatted for almost an hour-and-a-half. Ii felt like I was talking to the same girl I used to talk three years ago. In fact, this time, we had a lot to catch up on, since we hadn't been in touch for far too long. I was still not able to figure out why she tried to contact me, but I felt a lot better.

In the meanwhile, I got a message from Faiyaz, "Where are you?"

I replied, "Main gate teashop."

"Coming in two minutes."

Faiyaz came in less than two minutes and we ordered tea.

He asked, "What happened? Where did you disappear all of a sudden? I was searching for you on the entire floor, then Aniket told me you had taken a break."

I took a sip of my tea, "Yes, I called up Anushka."

He was surprised, "What? You mean that girl from your school love story about whom you had told me?"

"Yes."

"But you told me that you have no contact with her?"

"Yes, but yesterday she called me up."

"Yesterday?"

Faiyaz was getting one surprise after another. I answered, "Yeah, she called me up when we were all in the multiplex yesterday."

"Okay, that's the reason you went out after intermission."

"Yes."

"But why after two years?"

"I don't know, and that was the reason I was disturbed. So I requested Aniket to give me a break."

"So did you get your answer?"

"What answer?"

"Yehi ki, all of sudden this surprise call?"

"No."

"You could have asked her."

"Dude, I can't ask her directly, but I will find out."

"So you mean to say, you will keep in touch with her and re-kindle your relation again?"

"I don't know; I mean, I really don't have an answer."

Faiyaz got a bit irritated listening to this, "Aryan, she didn't care a bit for you and your feelings only because you future seemed bleak and shallow back then, and now she's back on the game. Can't you see? Grow up, buddy!"

I appreciate how Faiyaz cares about me. I was not offended. Whatever he said was regrettably true.

I smiled at him to make the situation less bothersome, "Don't worry."

He just gave a peculiar smile, clearly indicating he didn't like whatever had happened.

7

A short review of the next eight months

A lot of things happened in the next eight months. It is tough to find words to express my feelings on a piece of paper.

Anushka and I were back to our ritual of constant conversations over the phone. But this time, unlike when we were in high school, we would chat late at nights, only because of my shift timings.

My friends would pretty much get annoyed with the fact that whenever we were out over the weekends, I would fiddle with my phone.

My father did not fancy the way I had described Anushka.

Three months passed. Anushka and I decided to take a phone connection with some attractive STD calling scheme. Surprisingly, she was the first to purchase the mobile and kept shouting at me why I had been delaying the same.

Valentine's Day
I don't know how many of you understand the concept of what we have been celebrating on the 14th of February – Valentine's Day (kiss and hug complimentary).

St. Valentine was a Roman who was executed for refusing to give up Christianity. He died on February 14, 269 A.D., the same day that had been devoted to love lotteries. Legend also says that St. Valentine left a farewell note for the jailer's daughter, who had become his friend, and signed it "From Your Valentine." Other aspects of the story say that St. Valentine served as a priest at the temple during the reign of Emperor Claudius. Claudius then had Valentine jailed for defying him. In 496 A.D., Pope Gelasius set aside February 14 to honor St. Valentine.

It was Valentine's Day and luckily a Saturday, which meant a weekend off for me. No office, no college, but unfortunately, no girlfriend. Okay not exactly no girlfriend; I can say girlfriend under consideation!

I decided to wish Anushka but wasn't sure; after all, she had a boyfriend.

It sounds strange but though we two talked frequently, I had never asked her about her boyfriend. She was good looking and mature who believed in commitment, so it should be a special day for her. Rupam might have come down from Bangalore to Delhi just to spend some quality time with her, I thought.

I thought, "Enough of permutation and combination, I can just call her and simply wish her. Nothing to feel bad." I realized the person within me was a hundred times more intelligent and mature than the person everyone knew from the outside.

I finally called her up.

"Hi Anushka."

"Hey, what's up?"

"Good, happy Valentine's Day, dear."

"Same to you."

I tried to smile and asked her, "So what's your plan for today?"

After a few seconds of silence she replied, "Well, nothing much. I am at home only. It's Saturday, so no college."

"How dull and boring!"

"I know," I could sense something was wrong, because abruptly her voice went down.

I got a bit curious and thought of asking her. "Well, you should be going for a date today with Rupam, right? I am sure he's come from Bangalore?"

There was dead silence from her end.

"Hey, you there?"

This time, with a real disappointed tone, she replied, "Yeah, tell me, I am listening."

Maybe I had asked something I shouldn't have. I apologized, "Hey dear, I am sorry if I've offended you."

She immediately responded, "Hey, no Aryan, don't be sorry. It's just that…"

"Is everything alright? I mean, if you want you could talk to me."

She said, "I don't know how to share this thing with you."

I was curious, "Why, what has happened?

"Okay listen, I broke up with Rupam about a year-and-a-half back. I wanted to share this with you but…"

"Are you serious or kidding?" I was really surprised.

"Does it look like I am joking?"

"No…"

"Well, I moved to Delhi, he came once to meet me and gave me the news that he was dating one of his colleagues. That was the last time we met … That's all."

"But why? You are a good girl and you both were committed to each other."

"I know, I was ready but he was not confident about long distance relationships so he started seeing someone else."

I just spoke in anger, "Now this is insane, man! I mean, you are a wonderful girl. Infact, prefect ... is he blind?"

"That's what *you* think, not *him*"

"Bloody fucker!" That was a spontaneous reaction.

She was surprised "Excuse me?"

I checked my language, "Sorry, but there is no better way of describing him."

"Chuck it, Aryan. I am out of it and I am doing well now..." she tried to smile but sounded very artificial. "Hey, so what's your plan?"

There was a broken heart behind that artificial smile, ready to cry out to the whole world, and especially to me. I so wished I could have given her a tight hug.

It was clear that she was trying to change the topic; I didn't stretch.

I replied, "Nothing as such; might go out for a movie ... late night."

"Hmm. I see ... girlfriend, huh?"

"I am not that lucky ... Will go out with Faiyaz and the gang," She knew about my super crazy friend circle.

She tried pulling my leg ,"How boring Aryan! Find a good girl for you rself ... Do you want me to help you out?"

I laughed and replied, "Thank you so much, but I am happy."

"Are you sure?"

"Of course, I am."

"A little," she smiled.

"Flirting, huh?"

"With you? Gone mad..."

"Why, am I that bad?"

"I know, but I cannot flirt with you."

"Yeah, but why?"

She replied in a semi-rough tone, "Shut up, Mr. Sherlock Holmes."

"Okay."

I was getting a call on wait. I looked at the number, talk of the devil; it was Faiyaz.

I told her, "Hey dear, can I call you back? Getting call another."

"Sure."

The proposal

It was "Thanksgiving day" in the United States, so got an additional off from work. What a month! It was a Friday, so three consecutive holidays. I so wished the Americans celebrated thanksgiving every month, which would always be on a Friday or a Monday.

For a change, I thought of taking my parents out for dinner. After much thought, I shortlisted "*Sajha Chula*" located in the Eastern, Metropolitan Bypass. It's an air-conditioned Punjabi *dhaba* where you will get the best Biryani and kebabs in Kolkata.

We had just finished our starters and were waiting for the main course to arrive. I felt my cell phone vibrating in my jeans pocket.

It was a message from Anushka – "Please call me back, it's urgent."

I came out of the Dhaba and dialled her number.

"Hi."

"Hello sweets," she smiled.

I tried to be sarcastic, "*Kya baat hai*, someone sounds too romantic today."

"Really?"

"Yeah, tell me what happened?"

"Nothing."

"Then, why did you send the message?"

"Just like that. Where are you now?"

I felt a bit irritated, I had left my parents in the middle of dinner thinking something was wrong. "I came to *Sajha Chula* with my parents for dinner."

"Are you angry, Aryan?"

"No, why?"

"Nothing, I just wanted to tell you that I really like you."

That didn't surprise me much, because all the words she uttered were jumbled up.

I asked her, "Anushka, are you drunk?"

She gave a bizarre smile and replied, "*Arre waah!* You caught me."

"Yes, because you sounded like that. What happened all of a sudden?"

"Nothing, Ronit came to my place with a bottle of Vodka and we just had two shots. But I am not all that drunk"

I never heard about this friend of hers, so just avoided asking who she is. Might be one of her college friends.

"Okay, so you had a good time, I guess."

She again gave that weird smile, "Yeah, but I am missing you and I really like you, Aryan but..." she stopped.

I asked, "But what?"

"Nothing, just that you are very immature and younger to me."

I really didn't know what to say, "Well, living in the twenty-first century, you are bringing that age-story up again? And all of a sudden, what happened?"

In a petulant voice, she replied, "I don't know, I was missing you. So thought of hearing your voice."

I was wondering what I would say about this to my parents and saw a call waiting in my cell phone, "Dad is calling."

"Hey Anushka, they are waiting for me. Can I call you back later?"

"Okay."

"And yeah, don't drink much. I will return home and call you if you are awake."

"I will wait for your call."

Dinner was good and my parents were very happy, but somewhere in my mind, I was lost in some other world. I thought about her all along, wondering why she would pick me to call up when she was semi-drunk.

She told me she was missing me. I had often heard that human beings tend to speak the truth when they're drunk, mostly. Shall I assume that she was falling for me? I don't think so. According to her, she needed a mature man and someone elder to her, so I did not qualify anyway.

Just one philosophy sometimes really bothered me right from my high school days. Is it a real big crime if a girl expects her man to build the entire world for her and fulfill all her happiness, rather than creating it all by her? Most of the time, the girl who went by this philosophy was considered an opportunist; that's what even I thought Anushka to be, two years back when she revealed about Rupam. But honestly, it's very difficult to come to a conclusion if this philosophy was good or bad.

Three months later
The three months that followed were dreamtime for me .We chatted a lot and friendship was attempting to turn the tables. She was in a confused state of mind.

Whenever I planned to visit her in Delhi, she always refused. How I wish I could hold her, touch and feel her. Look into her beautiful eyes and let her know that I'm always there for her.

Friends were not happy with my growing intimacy with Anushka, especially Faiyaz. He always warned me, "*Bhai*, think before you act."

One day I asked her, "Anushka, don't you find anything special in me? I mean, can't we plan to think about our future jointly?"

She thought for a while and answered, "*Dekho* Aryan, you are a very good guy. In fact, the person who stands beside me every time and anytime but somehow you know, you are still a lot shaky taking your decisions. I mean, you lack maturity. Tell me something, why don't you look for a good girl for yourself?"

This was really a clever move. Just to play safe, she gave me an option of seeing some other girl, even though she knew the truth.

The truth was, I had been trying to find another. I had tried a lot, dating college girls from my engineering college, girls from my workplace, but I always tended to compare them to Anushka.

Chances were less for me, but I always dreamt about her, as nothing was more real to me than my own dreams. I know the world could change around me, but not my dreams. I was the sole owner of it and no one could take it away.

Some girl who could sweep me off my feet should do, but till now, only Anushka Banerjee had qualified.

It was late in the evening on Sunday when I got a surprise. An sms flashed up on my mobile screen, "Hi Aryan, I am coming to Kolkata for two weeks for my vacations."

8

Love at Park Street

It was a good dream, but I felt someone was shaking my entire body. I opened my eyes. It was Faiyaz.

He smiled at me, "*Oye bhaisaab*, we reached your home and you were sleeping like you hadn't slept for the last two days."

Even the driver was staring at me, I noticed while looking at the looking glass. I don't know why, but like an idiot, I was staring at Faiyaz.

I never had the habit of sleeping in a car while returning home from the office, but today, it was an exception and thinking about Anushka, I almost dreamt everything.

I said, "Thank you" to the driver and came out of the car.

I was trying to open the main door of my house. Faiyaz said, "Dude, you were sleeping like a half dead man and making a movie plan with her."

I was opening the lock on the door. Without looking at him, I answered, "*Kaise pata chalega*? How could someone see oneself sleeping?"

Well, he was quiet after that, which means clean bowled. "Wow!" It's actually very difficult to beat him in verbal duels, but this time, I won.

We decided to rest for a while and once Anushka called after the movie, I thought of moving towards the park.

I was really excited to meet her; it had been more than two years.

About half an hour later, my phone rang.

"Hi , where are you?" she asked.

"I am at home, Anushka. So your intermission is over?"

"No, the movie is over. Now tell me where we will meet."

"Hey dear, you were suppose to call me after the intermission and not after the movie."

She smiled, "Oop! I am sorry. Now tell me when and where to meet."

"Ah! How about Park Street in an hour?"

"Okay, Park Street. Where?"

"In front of Music world."

"Okay, but please try to make it quick, Aryan. Both Kaira and I are very hungry. We haven't eaten yet."

"Okay, I will try to be there as soon as possible. Chalo bye."

"Bye."

Faiyaz and I got up after a short nap and came to the main road to hire a taxi. Approximately it would take forty-five minutes for me to reach Park Street. A funny incident happened here.

We boarded a taxi and after ten minutes, Faiyaz asked the taxi driver, "*Bhai saab apka shaadi hua hai kya?* Are you married?"

The driver turned around, smiled and replied, "*Han Saab, ek ladki bhi hai.*"

Faiyaz smiled and replied, "Very well, *aap jaldi gaadi chalaiye warna...*" looking at me, *"Yeh bhaisaab agar late hogaya to iska shaadi nehi hogi."*

I looked at him and said, "Shut up, dude." Although I was making a desperate attempt to control my laughter. Faiyaz and the driver laughed. I looked out of the window.

It was a similar feeling like I had in my high school days when I went to meet Anushka for the first time; the only difference being that I wasn't nervous anymore.

Park Street!

The street that never sleeps, that's what we call one of the most happening places in Kolkata. Park street – if one looks back in history books it has something else stored as a story which is hard to believe.

In the year 1767, the official burial ground within the St. Jones Church premises was facing a severe space crunch. It was on 25 August, 1767 when a new burial ground (South Park Street Cemetery) was built on Circular Road. Since then, the connecting road came to be known as the 'Road to Burial Ground'. The name 'Park Street' owes its origin to the deer park of Sir Elijah Impey, the first Chief Justice (appointed in 1773) of the New Supreme Court, then at Calcutta.

We both were fifteen minutes late, but couldn't help the traffic jam and you really cannot escape from it in a city like Kolkata.

I called Anushka up, "Hey! Where are you?"

"Waiting for you where you asked me to for the past half an hour," she replied.

Now this is unfair; I was just fifteen minutes late.

I protested, "Who told you to come early? I am only a few minutes late."

"Now shut up and tell me where you are?"

"I'm just about to walk towards the place; will reach in another two minutes."

"Okay," we disconnected the phone.

Faiyaz didn't utter a single word. Time to time, he would just look at me and smile like a total *kamina*.

As I was walking down, I noticed two girls standing in front of Music World.

I might fall short of words to describe this. Anushka was looking totally different. Time does such wonders, one can't even imagine. I mean, she was looking so gorgeous, at least different from the girl I knew two-and-a-half years back.

Long, healthy, shiny hair, semi-green contact lenses, which was looking very good with her profile, slim and toned body with a feminine physique. Kaira was also standing beside her.

As she saw me coming, I saw a bright smile on her face. She gave me a little hug, "Hi Aryan, after a long time."

I smiled and replied, "Yeah, it has been long."

"You look so different; apart from sounding like a kid over the phone, I can see some mature looks in you now."

"*Accha,* thank you very much," I looked at Kaira standing beside Anushka. "Hey Kaira, *aamchi* Mumbai after a long long time. How are you doing?"

She laughed and replied, "I am fine. How are you?"

"Doing pretty good, still alive."

Out of excitement, I almost forgot Faiyaz was with me. I apologized to everyone and looking at Faiyaz I said, "I am so sorry, this is my friend Faiyaz."

Faiyaz smiled and shook hands with Anushka, "Hi."

Anushka replied, "Hi Faiyaz, heard a lot about you from your friend."

Faiyaz then said a warm "Hi" to Kaira and she too reciprocated.

Anushka was looking totally different and so was Kaira. I had seen her once in their school and this girl looked totally different now. One advantage was that she had a good height and a very fair complexion. Wearing a cream sleeveless top with a matching black capri, she looked stunning and angelic. I felt she must have been modelling as she was actually looking like those girls on the ramp.

Anushka looked at me and said, "Aryan, we are very hungry. Have you had lunch?"

"Nope not yet, what do you want to have girls?"

She laughed, "Food."

"Good to hear that, what kind though?"

"Anything."

I looked at Faiyaz, "Trincas *chale,* Faiyaz?"

He replied, *"Chal."*

Four of us crossed the road and went to the other side. *Trincas is located just below the Hotel Park – one of the oldest bar cum restaurans on Park Street. Every evening they organize a live band show with different blend like blues, pop, jazz, etc. I don't know for sure but have heard from many people that some famous singer like Usha Uthup and Anjan Dutta started their singing career in this place some twenty to twenty-five years back.*

The restaurant is usually very crowded and even then, ome band was performing old Bollywood numbers. Before entering Trincas Faiyaz just whispered in my ears, *"Sahi hai beta,* not bad!"

I just looked at him and smiled.

9

Exotic lunch @ Trincas

We ordered our lunch, the late afternoon one, in fact.
I like to talk a lot, like talking is something that I can't do without. But somehow since high school, after meeting Anushka, I've grown to the habit of keeping quiet whenever she was around.

Faiyaz and I were sitting together and on the opposite side sat Anushka and Kaira.

Faiyaz started the conversation, "So Anushka, for how long are you going to be here in Kolkata?"

She smiled and replied, "Well just a week or so." Then looking at me and again back to Faiyaz, "Tell me something Faiyaz, is your friend really so calm and quiet all the time"

Faiyaz looked at me and gave me a weird smile, "Not at all. In fact, he speaks more than I do most of the time."

"Really, because I literally have to pinch Aryan to talk."

Well actually it was true so I just smiled and remained quiet.

My dear friend Mr. Faiyaz Khan is a champion in talking to girls, which I've always known and once again I got to watch his skills with pleasure. Somehow he was busy in conversation with some topic or the other with both the girls.

I was pretty quiet but finally, decided to say something. Kaira was sitting just opposite me. I asked her, "So Kaira, what do you do in Mumbai? Are you studying or working?"

She replied, "Just completed my air-hostess training from Frankfinn and I'm now trying for a job in all the airlines."

"Okay, I thought so."

"I beg your pardon?"

I smiled, "No, I mean when I saw you for the first time today after years, I thought you must be doing something glamorous like modelling and all that."

She didn't reply, just smiled gently. The attitude from school time was still there.

In the meanwhile Faiyaz got busy talking to Kaira. He had been in Mumbai for four years before joining Wipro in Kolkata, so he started off talking about Mumbai and I noticed Kaira was replying with lots of enthusiasm. It seemed, she loved Mumbai a lot.

Anushka would look at me and sometimes give me a cute little smile. I was looking at her and trying to ask her in sign language what was wrong with her.

While cutting the fish fry with her knife and fork, Kaira spoke out, "Aryan, I need help from you."

I asked, "Yep sure, tell me. What can I do for you?"

"Anushka was telling me you were very good at selecting appropriate gifts for just anyone."

I looked at Anushka and with a smile, I said, "Thank you Ma'am."

She smiled and replied, "You are welcome, sir!"

Kaira continued, "I want a suggestion for a gift for my boyfriend's birthday next month."

I asked, "Is he working?"

"Yeah, he is a businessman, runs his own company."

"Hmm, then I'm sure he is into formal dressing most of the time?"

She smiled and replied, "Now please don't give me the idea of gifting him cuff links."

That was simply awesome. How come she knew what gift I was about to mention. For a few seconds I started thinking, "Am I that predictable?"

"How about a laptop bag?"

She thought for a while and replied, "Not bad, thanks Aryan."

"You are most welcome."

Faiyaz asked Anushka, "Hey, so what's the plan after this?"

Anushka looked at me and in a petulant voice said, "Aryan, I want to drink up, please."

Oh man! That tone was too cute ... how could I deny?

I replied, "Okay, you can order a drink here."

"Can we go to some other place? This place is good for food, not drinks."

Faiyaz looked at me and asked, "Aryan, let's go to Opium, what say?"

I replied, "Not a bad idea."

Coming out of the restaurant, we walked towards the Park Street junction to get a taxi from the stand and also saw some of hand pulled rickshaws. These so-called Chinese inventions were being stalled to take commuters from Park Street to New Market through Free School street. That reminded me of some old childhood memories related to rickshaws and my mother. I still recalled my early school days – after getting down from the bus, my house was a ten-minute walk but roads used to be blocked by rain water. That's when this rickshaws became my school shoes saviours during rainy seasons.

During the late 19th century, it was the Chinese traders who introduced these hand-pulled rickshaws in Kolkata and later on when the city was the British capital, it was turned into a cheap mode of transport by the Englishmen.

We got into the taxi from Park Street junction and headed towards Salt Lake.

Opium is located near my office. It is a good pub with dim lights, ideal ambience especially for couples. And above all, they play some very good music.

Faiyaz was sitting in the front of the taxi; at the back Anushka was sitting between Kaira and me.

Throughout the journey from Park Street to Salt Lake, she kept tickling me. It was fun, no doubt, but there was a time when fun turned into irritation.

10

Booze @ Opium

The ambience at Opium was good as usual. Dim lights with good music, pocket-friendly menu card, what else would you wish for?

Faiyaz was sitting beside Anushka and Kaira and I sat opposite to them.

I decided not to drink and Anushka was totally in the mood to. She ordered a large Smirnoff vodka for herself along with Faiyaz and Kaira, while I just stuck to a chilled Thums Up!

Anushka asked Faiyaz, "So Faiyaz, I am very sure your friend told you a lot about me."

Faiyaz took a sip of vodka and answered, "Yes, half of the day he talks only about you."

Anushka looked at me and stared. I just smiled.

She continued, "So I guess he said all good things?"

"Oh yes, but I am a bit disappointed."

"Why?"

I looked at him cautiously. I was sure he was about to throw a bullet from his mouth and I was correct.

"Yeah, Aryan used to say, she is one of the most beautiful girls I have ever seen in my entire life and all."

She smiled a bit and asked, "So according to you I am not beautiful, right?"

"Well, I never said that. But you are not as beautiful as my friend said. But you are good."

That was too harsh; it a hit out at me too.

I just looked at Anushka's face, it looked pale. She was beautiful, no doubt, and conscious of it. All of a sudden, if someone comments this way about a girl, it will definitely create volcanic bubbles in her mind.

Everyone was quiet for a few seconds. I tried changing the topic, "Guys, any more vodka?"

Anushka looked at me. She looked serious, "One large for me."

I looked at Faiyaz. He said, "Repeat Bhai."

Finally I turned my attention towards Kaira. She was still holding her glass with seventy percent of vodka in it. She smiled and said, "I am fine Aryan, thank you."

Thank god, second round of Smirnoff worked. The topics and discussion changed and it was pretty fine. Kaira went out for a few minutes as she got a call. I believed it was from her boyfriend. I remember Anushka telling me about Kaira dating this one guy in Mumbai.

After Kaira came back, we exchanged places; Anushka came and sat beside me.

She smiled, so I looked at her and asked, "What happened?"

"Why, can't I look at you?"

"Sorry, you can."

"Better be, dear. One more Vodka for me."

This was going to be her third large shot. I was not able to figure out why she was drinking so much and with so much aggression. Maybe she had changed after staying in Delhi.

We ordered a Vodka for her. She was looking different and beautiful, rather hot with those tipsy eyes staring at me.

She finished off the vodka in just one shot. That was awesome! For the first time in my life, I got to see a girl so thirsty for drinks.

One little burp and then a weird sound, she literally banged the glass on the table to keep it down.

I looked at the glass and then at her, "That was too hard Anushka, is everything alright?"

She smiled at me, "Can I ask you something?"

"What?"

"Why do you like me so much? I mean there are so many good girls out there, why me?"

I took a sip of my cold drink and replied without looking at her, "Well that's my problem now, I'm not so desperate so as to run after girls."

She was not convinced as it was difficult to convince a half-drunken girl.

She asked me again, "But why me Aryan? Don't be so good to me, please."

I didn't answer, just put on a strained smile.

In the meanwhile, one more round of Vodka came for Anushka and Faiyaz. Kaira was still sitting and talking to Faiyaz with that first glass of Vodka. It's either that she is not used to alcohol or she was not comfortable drinking with us.

I was still trying to figure out why she was asking me all the weird questions which neither had a head nor a tail.

Anyway, Opium didn't turn out to be very good. Everything was going well, but Anushka was absolutely drunk. She was not able to get up from the couch when we were about to move out. Thank god Kaira was with her or else it would have been difficult for me to control her. I had never experienced this type of situation before.

Getting a taxi was not difficult outside the pub. It was again Anushka sitting between me and Kaira and Faiyaz in front beside the driver.

11

A shocking journey

The traffic was really slow in some places on EM Bypass and you should have seen Anushka. She was going on singing one song after another, looking out of the window and sometimes looking at me and Kaira. But there was complete silence amongst the four of us, except for her singing. I noticed the taxi driver staring at her.

We decided to drop Kaira first, then Anushka. I asked Kaira, "Hey, so where shall we drop you?"

She looked at me and replied, "Haltu, Dhakuria."

I looked at the Taxi driver and said, "Dada, Haltu." He nodded.

The Eastern Metropolitan bypass road looks beautiful after sunset with some food-joints, dhabas , Science City, the massive ITC Sonar Bangla Hotel, Silver spring club and many more constructions going on both sides of the road. This bypass road is twenty kilometres approximately, along the eastern rim of the city and considered to be one of the most important roads of Metropolitan Kolkata, connecting several major junctions like Gariahat, Park-Circus, etc. But right now, the road was pretty messed up due to Metro Rail constructions.

Well, the best way to console myself about the terrible condition of the road was, 'This is for our better future, huh!

The taxi crossed the Science City bridge and another small surprise came my way. The taxi driver had AMAR FM playing in his music player and a very famous Bengali track came on the radio "*Telephone*" by Gautam Chatterjee. Anushka literally lifted both her hands on top and started singing the song – *Aashai aashai boshe aachi*. The side effect of suppressed excitement, her elbow came and hit my jaws.

"Ouch," I groaned and looked at her. She had not even realized what had just happened.

Kaira was trying to catch hold of her dancing hand, "Chill Anushka, what are you doing?"

But, she was in her own world.

Meanwhile, the taxi reached Ruby Junction. The driver looked back and asked me, "Dada, where in Haltu do you wish to go?

Like Newton's third law, I looked at Kaira and asked, "Kaira, can you give directions?"

A big question on Kaira's face. With a very innocent smiled she answered, "Aryan, I stay in Haltu at my Mashi's place, but all I can remember now is that there is a mosque near my Mashi's house."

Just guess, what would be the reaction listening to this. I felt like banging my head on the window of the taxi door.

Faiyaz was sitting in the front. He turned back. I guess Kaira felt a little awkward; she gave a sweet smile and said, "Sorry guys, I am not from Kolkata. I just remember the landmark, I am really really sorry."

A pretty girl knows, giving an innocent smile in front of a guy is an undefeated weapon. Well, the same worked for me and Faiyaz. I told the taxi driver, "Dada, you take left from the Siemens building towards Haltu; I will ask someone."

He nodded again and continued driving. Oh god, I had completely forgotten about Anushka. She now stopped singing and asked Kaira, "Honey, why are we going to Haltu? My house is at Jadavpur."

I must appreciate the patience level of Kaira. She replied in a polite tone, "Aryan will drop me and then he will drop you home."

She touched my cheek, "Thank you Aryan, so sweet of you."

I removed her hand from my cheek and said, "Now sit quietly, we need to find the house."

She partially obeyed me by not talking to us, but went back to singing songs again.

Meanwhile, the taxi took a left turn from the Siemens office. This road went straight to Haltu, we had to ask about the mosque.

On the way, the taxi driver asked a couple of people walking on the road about the mosque. I asked Kaira, "Are you able to figure out the direction?"

Looking out of the window she told, "I think yes Aryan, we are going in the right direction."

I was quiet for a moment thinking, did my day go well or did it get worse than I thought? One thing I was sure of, after we drop Anushka, Faiyaz Khan was going to take my class royally.

Almost after twenty-five minutes of searching, finally Kaira said "Bhaiyaji, take a left and stop."

Phew, she figured out her Mashi's place. The taxi took a left turn and we saw the mosque. This was the first time I had come to Haltu, though I had heard about this place from my mother once.

Kaira gave Anushka a hug with some girl talk in a low voice and got down from the taxi. Me and Faiyaz did the same.

I was leaning on the door of the taxi. She came near me and said, "Aryan, she is drunk. Please drop her home safely." And then looking at me and Faiyaz, she smiled, "And again a big sorry for forgetting the route to my house."

Faiyaz Khan finally opened his mouth after a long silence, "*Koi nehi*, it happens. We are lucky that a beautiful girl like you managed to spend some extra time with us."

Kaira just gave a gentle punch on Faiyaz's arm, smiled and said, "Shut up now. Don't exaggerate!"

Suddenly, I saw Anushka's face, looking at the three of us and figuring out what we were talking about, "What are we waiting for? Any more plans?"

Kaira looked at her and said, "No baby, you will be dropped home by Aryan."

Before Kaira could say anything, I went a little close to her and said in a calm voice, "Thanks Kaira for joining us; it was a real pleasure."

The next thing she did was unexpected. She gave me a hug and said, "No need to be formal. You are always welcome," then looking at me, " Listen take my phone number and give me a call once you drop her home, okay?"

I smiled and replied, "Okay ma'am, your wish is my command."

We exchanged numbers and left for Jadavpur; fortunately Anushka was quiet all this while.

The taxi driver must have wondered what was going on.

The road from Haltu to Jadavpur goes via Dhakuria. *Oh yes, Dhakuria is a known place to me as I come to Dakshinapan to hang ont with my band-mates sometimes. There is a panipuri wala who sits in front of Dakshinapan gate, and trust me folks, I am sure he makes the best panipuri in the city.*

The taxi was goings through the narrow roads with people walking on both sides, loads of shops around along with the autorickshaw stands at many places.

There was complete silence. Anushka's silence was bothering me, but not for a very long time.

Out of the blue, she said looking out of the window, "Aryan, why don't you just leave me?"

I was not ready for such a comment. Totally floored, I asked in a surprised tone, "What?"

Now she looked at me, she looked pretty normal now. Without even blinking her eyes she said again, "Why is it so difficult for you to understand? You just go away, try and forget me, please."

No proper sleep, dramatic evening and now this....

I felt completely helpless. Looked at the front, Faiyaz was listening to music on his headphones. The taxi reached Dhakuria and took a left turn from the junction towards the Jadavpur Police Station.

A minute of silence followed. I tried holding her hand but instantly got a slap on my left cheek. Shocked, I couldn't believe it myself that she had slapped me. She uttered the same thing in a rough tone again, "Just leave me and go, Aryan."

I felt like crying, but it got stuck somewhere. In a shaky voice, I asked, "What have I done Anushka?"

"Nothing, you did not do anything. That's your problem; you are actually too innocent to do anything. Please, I beg of you, leave me and find a better girl."

The taxi had reached Jadavpur 8B bus top. I tried to be very normal and told the driver, "Dada, take a right and go straight."

Another two minutes leter, I told the driver to stop in front of an apartment. She opened the door and I followed her.

She came towards me and said, "Bye Aryan, take care."

In response, I asked, "Are you okay now?"

I was getting surprised by her every minute; her sudden change of behaviour was upsetting. She looked at Faiyaz and said, "Bye Faiyaz, it was nice meeting you."

Faiyaz was still sitting inside the taxi. Putting down his headphone, he looked at Anushka and replied with a smile, "Thanks, bye bye."

No more conversation. She walked away and I was standing there like a stone for the next couple of minutes.

Many a time, William Shakespeare's Romeo and Juliet *inspired me to think what an epic love they had. But my current condition de-motivated me to such an extent that my heart and mind revolted together against this immortal epic.*

Didn't realize when Faiyaz came out of the taxi and stood beside me. He asked, "Shall we go now?"

Without saying anything to him, I sat inside the taxi and told the driver, "Dada, leave us till Gariahat Signal."

Faiyaz now came and sat beside me.

The taxi went till Jadavpur 8B bus-stop and took a left turn towards Dhakuria. Faiyaz broke the silence and asked me, "Do I need to ask you anything?"

I just looked at him and again looked out of the window without responding to what he had asked.

He lit a cigarette without commenting anything at my reaction.

After getting down from the Dhakuria Bridge, there was a bit of congestion at the Gol Park Signal. Nothing new as it's one of the busiest junctions of South Kolkata.

He looked at me and asked, "Want to wait in this traffic or walk down towards Pantaloons?"

I replied, "Let's walk."

I paid the fare and both of us got down in front of Ramakrishna Mission, Gol Park. We often go to the tea shop at the exit-door of Pantaloons, Gariahat and chit-chat there for hours.

In evening time, Gariahat makes a shopaholic feel like a kid let loose in a candy store. With numerous shops on both sides of the main road and hawker-occupied pavements, this place provides a completely different shopping experience in entire Kolkata, especially the bargaining part. Above all, it's Kolkata and everyone knows bongs love eating junk food. So a shopping experience feels incomplete without snacks; puchkas, samosas, kathi *rolls, fish-fries and the list goes on.*

After a very long break, while walking down the pavement towards Ballygaunge, I lit a cigarette. The silence went beyond my control and I spoke, "Yaar, why did she behave so badly?"

Faiyaz ha been quiet all this while, but suddenly he got furious, "WTF is your problem? Are you an idiot or you don't want to understand deliberately?"

To be frank, I was not at all surprised by this sudden display of anger. I had seen it coming. It's true, maybe I didn't want to understand and somewhere it was hurting my credibility of being honest. This was the first surprising misbehaviour from Anushka.

I did not reply. We reached the exit gate of Pantaloons. The chaiwala's shop was open and crowded as always; ordered chais and sat on the bench outside the shop.

Faiyaz lit a cigarette, took the first puff and looked at me, "Will you please say something?"

Taking a sip of chai I replied, "Don't know, my mind is not working."

"Dude, do you have a dignity of your own or have you sold it somewhere? Why the hell are you wasting your time? She told you what she had to say. Grow up man." One more puff of cigarette, "You have better things to do in your life."

It's true, truth and reality are very hard to digest and it's human nature to struggle before accepting the fact. I'm no exception. Tears started falling from my eyes. I tried a lot to stop them, but failed.

War does kill thousands of people on the battlefield, but today the humiliation killed and crushed millions of charming dreams within my broken heart.

It took sometime for me to come back to normal. I decided, I would try my best not to be in touch with her. The little voice inside me said, "There are better things to do in life."

Enough of drama; it was time to return home.

12

Devil inside

A week passed by in its own tempo. I promised myself not to call up Anushka. There is an unambiguous added reason for it. I received an Orkut update that she was in Delhi. Damn! She went back without informing me.

I was at home, reluctant and irritated. My parents demonstrated their discomfort with my reaction and behaviour. When I went to the office, I tried my best to act normal. I was convinced that it was only a momentary phase.

It was Friday and my bad mood was awarded with another unanticipated client call. After all was done, I came back home in the afternoon, completely distressed.

Ours is a household of working parents, rather hard working parents. Their career has been equally and importantly balanced along with raising us and portraying a happy family life. They were still at work when I got back. After lazing around for some time, I took my lunch from the top shelf of the refrigerator. Inattentive and lost somewhere, I heated the food and kept the rest back. Thanks to my mom, I have my tummy full and my mind fuller.

Still dazed, I had just finished my lunch and had prepared to grab some sleep when I got a call from Faiyaz.

"Hello dada, *ki korcho?*"

"Nothing much, just had lunch. Preparing to take a nap."

"Very good." He said, "I will not chew up your time now, make sure you wake up in time to meet up at Gol Park Café Coffee Day at 6 p.m., Okay?"

Without any information, whenever this guy asks me to wait somewhere, it has always been an awaiting shocker for me.

"Why? Who is coming?"

"Kaira invited you."

Unbelievable, Faiyaz Khan!

"What did you just say?"

"Mr. Deaf, you heard me all right."

Faiyaz came across with his share of excuse, "I called her up just to say hi, and she said she is going to Gol Park with her friends and wants us to join."

"If that is so, she could have called and invited me herself. By the way, in between all these, how did you manage to get her number?"

"From your cell phone," He laughed.

"Asshole!"

He laughed, "Thanks man, I know that!" (Took a deep breath) "Listen, be there on time."

My thoughts trailed again from the situation of facing her and being an uninvited guest. For a couple of seconds I felt odd accepting an invitation in such an indirect way. For all I know, this could be a drama built by Faiyaz. How very embarrassing.

I countered the so-called invitation after juggling around with the situation, "You carry on dude, I will be needed at home."

An expected appearance got articulated. "I cannot go and blend with four-five girls, and be crushed in their girl talk, so you better come down."

"Tell Kaira, you have accommodated yourself with some work and join me at home. You don't really have to meet them, you know."

But, hell I had forgotten. Bringing Faiyaz Khan down in conversation and winning a trophy is impossible for most people.

The idea went unattended. Stern as he was, "Listen, stop behaving like a child. Take your time to grab a good sleep and then come over. See you at 6, bye."

I heard the phone disconnect.

I woke up with my cell phone alarm ringing. While dressing up as per the order of Mr. Khan, I recapitulated a quote my father had told me once,

"We cannot change our past. We cannot change the fact that people act in a certain way. We cannot change the inevitable. The only thing we can do is play on the one string we have and that is our attitude."

I reached the place before time and checked my phone to see the time (I don't have the habit of wearing wrist watch) ... I was fifteen minutes early. I grabbed a ciggy and started walking towards Gol Park. I didn't know what kind of embarrassment was waiting for me.

One of the busiest traffic signals of South Kolkata is the place where I was standing then. I was struggling to cross the Ramakrishna Mission signal. Struggle is the key to success, eureka! I crossed the road, walked towards Mouchak Sweets and saw a much known baldy in front of the shop with a diet coke in his hand. Ah! There stood my friend Faiyaz Khan (with loads of surprises and maybe, embarrassment as an additional free package).

He looked at me and gave me a smile, "I knew you would come early."

I grabbed the diet coke from his hand and took a sip before saying anything, "I see, guess you understand too much these days."

He laughed, "Nothing like that *mere bhai*. Kaira has called and you wouldn't come, that's impossible."

This is a completely false accusation. I came to save him from the group of girls and look who's blaming who!

I objected, "Listen dude, it's nothing to do with Kaira. I mean I barely know her. I came only because you called me."

He patted my shoulder and with a smile, said. "Thank you for coming."

Girl's psychology: Guys should always wait for them and when finally the girl comes and says, "I am so sorry, I am late," he should give a fake smile (at least try to) and say, "That's perfectly fine."

A gang of girls arrived. God! Too many surprises in my life of late. Reminds me of a famous quote by Vernon Walters – "It is an endless procession of surprises. The expected rarely occurs and never in the expected manner."

13

Sub-concious devil comes alive within me

There were four girls in front of me, besedes Kaira. I barely recognized anyone. I will talk about the rest of them later, right now just Kaira. She looked stunning. The girl I saw in the pub the other day and the girl standing now in front of me were completely different from each other. Very simple dress – a white Kurta and a black shrug which came into the craze after Kareena Kapoor wore it in *Jab We Met*.

She smiled at both of us, "Hey guys, good to see you again." Looking at her friends, she introduced us, "Okay Aryan and Faiyaz, this is Rituparna, Somreeta and Deblina."

We exchanged greetings.

Faiyaz Khan, as usual, started showing his charm, "Wow wow wow! Four beautiful ladies ... what more could you ask for this evening." All of us laughed.

Rituparna and Debolina looked a little bulky and bubbly type, but Somreeta was an example of a pretty Bengali girl with a fair complexion. She was wearing a semi-brown salwar kameez. But Kaira was something different. She looked hot even in ethnic wear.

I was a little uncomfortable with the thought at the back of the mind that, there were four girls. I didn't know what to say. Faiyaz was busy talking to all her friends and although I was quiet, I had direct eye contact with Kaira .Her eyes, I must say, had something different in them; they had a certain indefinable spark which always said something with a gentle touch of mischief, passion and utter naughtiness.

A devil woke up within me and I got an idea.

Smiling at her I asked, "So what's the plan, Kaira?"

Before Kaira could reply anything, one of the bubbly ladies, Debolina, said in a childish voice, "We will go to Ballygaunge Haldiram's."

With an atrocious and naughty smile, Kaira said, "Well Mr. Aryan, you got your answer. So let's go." Turning towards her friends she said, "Let's go girls."

I had heard about Haldiram's, it's one of those new outlets in Ballygaunge where I'd never been. We got into a taxi – Faiyaz and I in front, the girls at the back seat.

The taxi took U-turn and got on to the Gariahat – Ballygaunge flyover.

Sitting next to each other, Faiyaz and I exchanged looks and he smiled at me instantly. He might have thought that I was getting bored, but the truth is, my feelings were mixed.

Girl's talk going at the back seat, Debolina spoke this time, "Aryan, I heard about you a lot during school days but never got a chance to meet you in person, until now."

I looked back and smiled, "Is it ... hmm."

The traffic after the flyover was slow. I looked out of the window towards Pantaloons; the crowd was pouring in due to the fifty percent off.

I felt someone breathing very close to my ears. A whisper came from Kaira, "Mr. Aryan, I think Deblina likes you."

I turned my head around. Her face was so close to mine I could feel her silent breathing, her silent eyes, a small, cute nose, wet pink lips. She was just a few inches away from me; I controlled myself I got a plan and had to execute it.

The new Haldiram's was as huge as the one located on V.I.P road near International airport closest to Dumdum – a very famous outlet for veggies, especially the Marwaris.

We all got inside the four storeyed huge glass building. While walking towards the counter, Somreeta asked, "So what does everyone want to eat?"

I was in the mood of drinking chilled beer and veggies here. Before anyone could speak, I replied "Just cold drinks." Everyone looked at me with a question mark on their faces, "I had a very heavy lunch, so you guys order." Looking at Somreeta, I said, "Come Somreeta, let's order the food."

Everyone told me and Somreeta what they wanted to eat. Kaira too came along with us while the rest of them went to the second floor to find places to sit. I noticed that Rituparna was an introvert. She didn't even utter a single word, but gave a few smiles every now and then.

It felt great to be walking with a beautiful and hot girl in a busy food outlet of Kolkata. I was about to pay, but Somreeta and Kaira didn't let me.Before placing the final order, Kaira looked at me and asked, "Are you sure, just a cold drink?"

I nodded.

To tell the truth, I never liked Haldiram's food. Sweets are good but the rest of the food items are cooked in too much ghee. Excess intake of ghee could really upset my stomach.

We all were sitting together on the crowded second floor. Faiyaz was wearing a round-necked blue t-shirt with a scorpion tattoo sneaking out from the sleeves of his left hand. Debolina noticed it and out of excitement, pointed her finger at Khan Saab's tattoo.

"Faiyaz, is that tattoo permanent?"

Faiyaz took a glimpse of his tattoo, looked at Debolina and said, "Yes, it is with a lifetime warranty."

Bloody liar! Both of us had gone to Esplanade to shop in New Market a week ago. Right outside Rahman store, one guy was making temporary tattoo for hundred rupees, and out of curiosity, he went for it. But seriously, the work was done so neatly, it was tough to figure out that it was not permanent.

In the meanwhile, devil's mind the execute pre-meditated plan.

Kaira was sitting next to me. I loked at her once and took out my cell phone to dial a number.

Cell phone screen displayed '*Calling Anushka.*'

A couple of rings, then floating came a known voice, "Hello."

"Hi Anushka, remember me?"

"Shut up, Aryan! What sort of an idiotic question is this?"

"Sorry sorry, how are you?"

"I am doing good, and you?"

"Pretty well and right now,I have a surprise for you."

"What?"

"Hold on for a second and guess this voice."

Kaira was engrossed in some discussion with others, I didn't pay attention to what the topic was.

I gently touched her left hand. She looked at me. I showed her the cell phone with my other hand and said, "Call for you."

She took my cell phone with a question mark on her face. With hesitation in her voice she said, "Hello?"

The call lasted for a few seconds. I was looking anxiously at Kaira, trying to figure out the conversation.

She handed over the phone to me, "She wants to speak to you."

I took the phone back with a smile. Kaira again got engrossed in conversation with others.

"Hi Anushka, so how was the surprise?"

No response over the phone. Again I asked, "Are you listening?"

A cranky and rude voice came from the other end of the line, "What are you doing with my friends?"

Devils were dancing in my mind, "She invited me."

Once again, silence on the other end of the line.

I tried to sound innocent, "Anushka, what happened?"

"Nothing, you carry on with your so-called friends. I will get back to you later."

Beep beep beep ... The line got disconnected.

Job done, Eureka!

Everyone paid extra attention to the conversation, especially whenever Faiyaz cracked jokes with charm. I was engrossed with a question for myself: Whatever that happened a while ago, was it right? She got offended, which I was sure of from her tone. It was nothing but revenge. Yes this was my way of taking revenge on Anushka. In fact, why should I regret at all? After all, whatever she had done to me was heartbreaking.

No regrets for allowing the devil's thought to hurt her because it felt good; I felt better after giving up all hope. Falling in love cannot be planned by anyone, but there could have been a better way of making someone understand. Her sudden change of behaviour was not only a surprise but it also raised a question in my mind about my credibility.

However, I had no regrets for my behaviour that day.

After spending almost two hours there, we decided to leave. Rituparna and Somreeta had to rush home. Deblina was going out on a date with her boyfriend. Kaira was free and the weird surprise pack Mr.khan spoke up, "Aryan, can you drop Kaira home?"

I tried my best to hide my irritation and asked, "Why, where are you going?"

"Tanveer texted me; I have to give my house key to him. You drop Kaira and call me."

Four girls standing in front of me and creating a scene was out of the question. I agreed.

This un-natural behaviour of Faiyaz forced me to think at the back of my mind *'wtf was this asshole thinking?'*

The ambasador taxi ride
After everyone left for their destination, both of us got into a taxi. I said, "Dada, Dhakuria."

Without saying anything, he turned on the metre and started driving. Roads were still packed with vehicles, although the intensity of traffic was less compared to the evening. The Gariahat – Ballygaunge flyover was a necessity; without it, passing the Gariahat and Gol Park junction during peak hours is no less than a mental and physical torture, especially if you are driving or standing inside a crowded bus.

A few minutes of silence later, Kaira spoke, "Aryan, thank you for coming."

I looked at her. The same smile always glowed on her beautiful face. I smiled back, "I should rather thank you for giving me such good company."

"Is it?"

"Yes."

No answer. We looked at each other and laughed.

She checked her cell phone, kept it inside the bag and looked at me. Minor seriousness in the voice, "By the way Aryan, you were supposed to call or text me after dropping Anushka home. Very bad." She looked outof the window.

Yes, I was supposed to keep her in the loop, but that evening after whatever happened, I was honestly not in a condition to remember anything.

I placed my hand on Kaira's thigh, "Hey, I am terribly sorry, dear."

She turned towards me; killer looks.

Just looks, no words. That made me uncomfortable. I asked with a smile, "What happened?"

When she didn't say anything I went on, "I am really sorry Kaira. My condition that evening was such that..."

Before I could finish she interrupted and said, "I understand Aryan, no need to apologize. Not your fault."

"Thank you," I responded.

She asked, "Is everything okay between you and Anushka now?"

"What do you mean?"

"When you didn't call, I called up Anushka and got to know that you guys had fought after dropping me home."

I kept silent.

"Aryan, you have a better life ahead. So move on, dude."

The effortless attempt of the adrenaline rush of speech surprised her, "Nothing is okay between us. Can we please drop this topic?"

She sounded adamant with a never give up attitude, "You should know something Aryan, but I don't know how to say it."

By now, I was sure there was something which I should know but did not.

The taxi stopped; I looked out. Both of us were so engrossed in the discussion that I didn't notice we had reached Dhakuria.

The discussion was interrupted. We got out of the taxi.

My heart started beating faster as my mind tried to guess the possible news Kaira was about to reveal to me.

I paid the taxi fare and asked Kaira, "Are you in a hurry?"

She shook her head, smiled and replied, "Not really."

"Can we sit in Dakshinapan for some time, if that's okay with you?"

She caught my hand and gave a massive smile, "Hey chill Aryan! You don't have to be so formal with me."

We looked at each other; crossed the road and went into Dakshinapan.

Sitting on the stairs of Dakshinapan's Madhusudan Macha for an Adda is an altogether different stress-buster for a Bengali. The environment around me that day seemed completely different, probably due to the suspense Kaira was about to break.

I took the initiative to start the discussion we had left half way in the taxi, "So you wanted to tell me something."

Her voice sounded a little low with a hint of seriousness, "Yes, but I'm wondering how to start and where to start."

"I know dear, you are going to tell me something earthshaking. Don't worry go ahead and just say it," I tried convincing her to get her out of the hesitation.

It worked, she started, "How much do you talk to Anushka on day to day basis?"

Taken aback by surprise I said, "We talk almost every day over the phone, but why?

Kaira went on with her pace, ignoring the question mark on my face, "Do you talk to her at night?"

"Yes, I do."

"Have you noticed anything bizarre?"

The curiosity within me started increasing with every minute. I tried my best to overcome it as best as I could. I replied, "No, nothing unnatural."

"Are you absolutely confident and sure?"

The intensity in Kaira's voice literally made me wonder whether I was answering her questions correctly. I tried to think for a moment. Bingo! Yes I figured something out.

"Yes Kaira, I don't know if this makes any sense but for a couple of weeks her phone's been busy around midnight."

She sounded very calm, "I knew it, just wanted to hear it from you."

I stared at her like an idiot with millions of questions revolving in my mind.

She kept her hand on my thigh; I kept my hand over her hand, "What is it Kaira? Please don't prolong this suspense anymore."

She took a deep breath and gave me a a piece of information that hit me like thunderstorm, "Aryan, Anushka is having an affair with someone."

I left her hand and looked at the sky above me. She came and sat a little closer to me.

I was still looking up with both my eyes closed. Kept on telling myself again and again, *"No tears again, no tears again Aryan"* I looked at Kaira and asked, "When did this happen? You know anything about it?"

She stood up and caught both my hands, "Come, let's take a walk."

We started walking past the entrance of Madhusudan Mancha towards Jodhpur Park.

As we were walking, Kaira narrated the entire incident to me.

"I don't know Aryan if you have ever heard from Anushka that she had a crush on a guy called Ronit from her school days. They did not date but it was a strong crush from her side, at least that's what I heard from my friends in school. When she was preparing for her higher secondary exam, something went wrong and she was not in touch with this guy. All we used to hear during that time was about you."

She stopped speaking. I looked at her and she asked, "Are you sure you want to listen to this?"

I just nodded.

She continued, "When she went to Delhi to pursue her career in Law, I guess in some fair or party she met Ronit again and they continued to keep in touch once again. I never asked her if you were aware about this, but from her behaviour I figured she had hidden this from you."

I didn't let her finish her part of the explanation, "So, she's really having an affair, huh?"

Kaira answered, "Listen to the entire thing and you will get the answer yourself."

I apologized, "Sorry, please carry on."

She continued, "You want to know why she was desperate to meet you?"

I looked at her. The question mark on my face indicated I did not.

"Ronit proposed to Anushka and she told him to talk to her parents."

Again for the second time I interrupted, "What the hell are you talking about?" I stopped walking.

Kaira walked a little ahead of me. She stopped and turned around, "Yes Aryan, the day you came along with Faiyaz, Ronit brought his parents to talk to Anushka's parents. She didn't want to stay at home and that's the reason you and I were both invited."

Gosh! I rememebered this name Ronit. I was trying to recollect where I had heard this name earlier. I recalled it now. One evening when I had taken my parents out for dinner, she had called me all drunk and I clearly remember that she had said that Ronit had got the drinks for her.

I did not want to reveal this to Kaira and pretended I had heard the name for the first time.

I said to her, "The difference is, you knew everything and I didn't."

"Yes, but don't take me wrong, Aryan. I was really feeling bad and guilty that day, knowing everything and not warning you ... It's just, she is a good friend of mine so..."

I didn't let her finish, "It's okay Kaira, I understand, you need not feel guilty about this."

Kaira came near me and gave me a quick little hug which was unexpected and much needed.

Tears and anger were both trying to burst out. I tried pushing my face as much as possible into Kaira's collar bone to suppress the emotional breakdown. She understood.

People were walking past us and staring.

Kaira caught both my shoulder and said in a commanding voice, "Listen to me now, Aryan."

I made my best effort to look normal.

She looked into my eyes and said, "Aryan, you are qualified, talented and a wonderful companion to be with. Just don't waste this stage of life and move ahead. I am sure some way better surprises and happy future is waiting for you."

In a soft tone I replied, "Thank you."

"You need not thank me. Be realistic and practical in life, Aryan. It will help you come out of odd things, trust me."

I heard everything she said but her particular words "Trust me" went straight somewhere deep within my mind and heart.

I was amazed to see the spectacular realistic sense within this girl, capability of strong convincing power with a mix and match of good looks and versatility. Like a deer getting caught helplessly by four or five tigers together, I too got caught in Kaira's million dollar trustworthy charms.

The entire Anushka chapter had undoubtedly messed up Aryan Roy's happiness with his surroundings, but Kaira seemed to be acting as a painter, busy making a colorful canvas painting within the not so happening surroundings.

My gut feeling made me want to do something vindictive to Anushka, like breaking her pride or something that would make her realize and regret her mistakes. The word slap recapitulated the bad memory of getting slapped on my way back from the Opium pub a couple of days back.

In a flash of second – I decided, *revenge* ... yes *revenge* it is indeed ... Not sure how? But yes that's what I want-to calm the storm reging in my mind and heart.

Both of us started walking towards the Dhakuria Bridge. I wanted to drop Kaira home but she did not want me to. Fortunately she got an auto. Before getting into the auto she said, "Be in touch, wonder boy."

I smiled with an artificial adobe expression and waved, *"Jo hokum, Memsahib."*

She flashed a bright smile.

No more complications,my mind was clear like a bright sunny morning sky, making me feel very happy from within.

Kaira had done a huge favour by telling me everything about Anushka. I owed her something. Little bit of emotions were alive for my so called love, but the truth revealed today killed that too. I felt sad but at the same time understood that there was no point thinking about this girl; she was better placed in the past and I firmly believe my future was different in a much better way. She was free to move on without any explanation as she was never actually mine that I should have the primal fear of losing her.

I took out my cell phone, called Faiyaz, "Bhai, could you spare an hour for me?".

To hell with Anushka! I needed a chilled beer.

14

Changes and Surprises

I woke up to see my head lying heavily on Faiyaz's sofa. I had got dead drunk the other night. I couldn't recall a thing. No puking though, that's something I hate to the core.

Before I move further, let me brief a bit about this pub in Park Hotel where I happened to perform once with our band: *This place was established 19 August, 1994 with a touch of British architecture. Apart from serving different flavours of drinks this place is famous for Live Band Show every evening and one can afford to miss the Saturday night beer with live band performance, especially when its Hip-pocket, Krosswindz, Anjan Dutta, Indian Ocean any other band perform. According to the Wikipedia survey - 3285 hours of Live music is played in this place which is highest anywhere in India and ranks among the top ten positions in Asia based on this category.*

There is a program called Open Mic Sessions which is held here once in every month. Any band or artist related to music/poetry /stand up comedy can perform.

When I got up, I recapitulated two things – Sitting on the footpath in front of Park Hotel, calling up my mom to inform that I was staying at Faiyaz Khan's place; and texting Kaira, "I miss you sweetheart."

Holy shit! I went through the text outbox again. Did I seriously send this message to her?

Yes, I had actually sent her the text and got a reply, "I was waiting to hear this from you, but boy you're slow. Lol! Jus kiddin. Enjoy your beer, cheers"

Faiyaz had already woken up and was sitting and reading the newspaper. I got up from the sofa and showed him the text. After reading it he gave a wicked smile, "What's up, dude? What's going on?"

Seriously, I myself didn't know what had made me do it, "I seriously don't know, excessive alcohol, may be."

He kept the newspaper aside, came and sat beside me, put his hand over my shoulder and said, *"Abe Bokachoda*, don't act like an innocent freak in front of me. You like her, right?"

I removed his hand from my shoulder and stood up, "No dude, I am yet to come out of the shock and you are assuming that I like her already?"

"Why? Which dictionary states that it's not possible?"

"No, I mean, maybe it's possible, but to me it's like, I don't know her well enough to like her just as yet."

"Listen here, if you don't know her, then you will surely come to know and..." He started giving that wicked smile again.

"And what?"

"And I guess, at least you have a crush on her."

I got irritated, "Oh come on, I am not in the mood to play around. I will call her up and say sorry."

"Don't!"

"Why?"

"Text her back again, tell her that you enjoyed last night's chat a lot but it would have been perfect if she were present. If you get a reply like 'I wish I could' would mean, she didn't mind you sending that text last night."

I stood silent for a few seconds and walked towards the kitchen. Time for some brew!

I felt a little awkward doing what my philosopher buddy had suggested to me. I was sure my mate would put me into some serious trouble someday.

This is how I framed my so called apology – "*Hey Kaira , you could sum up last night's incident by thinking that I was celebrating my independence day and got overly drunk. I have no idea when I texted you. You're really someone special and should have been in someplace else with me, but if that text offended you, I am really sorry. Have a blessed day ahead!*"

I went back home late in the afternoon and looked at my cell phone screen every now and then for a text to pop up. The whole day passed without a single text message from Kaira. I even thought of sending her more messages or maybe ring her up, but I controlled myself.

The weekend ended and the normal nocturnal working day started for me. It had been two days and there was neither any call nor any text from Kaira. I thought it over multiple times to give her a call and check; in fact, even made an attempt to but to my surprise, her cell phone was out of range. So, before logging off on Tuesday, I forwarded a text to her "Hey dear! Hope you're doing good, got a bit concerned as your phone is out of range."

It was Thursday, the day I usually feel energized mentally with the sense of happiness – Two more days and then the weekend starts.

After over a week, I had dinner with my parents. It's really very odd, staying in the same house and getting to meet my dad only during weekends. Couldn't help much with the routine though, it had gotten so monotonous – I came back from the office around 1 and after lunch, I went off to sleep. By the time I got up, it was.

Mom remain awake for some chit-chat and accompanies me for dinner, but dad used to sleep off.

That day, fortunately due to some office work, dad was awake and we got a chance to have dinner together on a weekday. After food, I went back to my room to rest for some time and heard my cell phone ringing.

There was a glaze on my face, looking at the cell phone display "Kaira calling."

With energy in my voice, I received the call, "Hello."

The same cute voice said, from the other end of the line "Hey Mr. Roy! What's up?"

A small fight continued over the phone:

"Nothing's up; just a white colored ceiling fan."

"That was not funny at all."

"Where the hell you have? Been trying your phone for the last three days?"

"*Aare bapre*, so much anger?"

"Naturally."

"Why?" she laughed.

"What do you mean by why?"

"I meant, why are you angry and concerned? Are you my boyfriend?"

"What?"

She smiled again, "I thought you missed me."

I surrendered in front of her smile, softened my voice and asked, "Now stop this and tell me, where have you been?"

She took a deep breath, "Well Aryan, there is good and bad news together."

I mentioned earlier in this story but once again, girls are champions in complicating any topic, not necessary that it makes sense or not.

"Why do you create so much of suspense? Be specific."

"Which one do you want to hear first?"

"As in?"

She answered in a non-Bengali accent, *"Mane, Aage kharap news sunbe tumi na bhalo news sun be?"* Do you want to hear the bad news first or the good one?"

It was the first time I had heard her talking in Bengali. It felt nice.

"Tell me the bad news first."

"I broke off with my guy," she kept quiet.

"What? I mean what happened?"

"He is getting married."

"Can I ask you something?"

"Sure Aryan, go ahead."

"I heard from Anuskha once that you were not committed to your guy, rather it was like an open relationship."

"Yes , you heard the right thing."

"Hmm so if you are okay, then tell me what happened."

Kaira narrated her story, "I met this guy around two years back through online chat. We started chatting together for nearly two or three months before meeting up. We liked each other, pretty jovial and straightforward guy who runs his own company." She stopped and confirmed if I was listening, "You there?"

"Yes, dear."

She continued, "We were seeing each other casually. You know, like watching movies, clubbing, long drives, dinner and all that stuff. One fine day he proposed. I thought for a day and said yes."

I interrupted, "Then why is he getting married to someone else?"

"When we started dating he told me that he comes from a very conservative Gujarati family and that love marriage was not even an option. Moreover, he is seven years older to me. I knew, he would get married within a few years, so we mutually opted for a casual relationship."

"But you guys could have given it a try?"

"My parents won't agree as I am too young and my career has just started."

"So why was your phone out of range for three continuous days?"

"For a few months Pratik's parents were looking for a suitable Gujrati match for him and for this, things were not going good between us. I knew this day would come so just to change my mood, I was in Kolkata..." she stopped.

Awkward situation! I was looking for words to console her, "I am sorry to hear that, dear. I wish I could help you out."

"So sweet of you Aryan, don't be sorry. I knew this day would come and it's okay. I don't regret anything."

"How can you be so normal Kaira?"

"I try and take life the way it comes and goes, and leave the rest to destiny. Applicable to you too dear ... Life will be a lot easier."

I've seen many breakups from my school days till now. The breakups in school always looked pretty casual to me, just a transition in every human being's life to maturity; the next level was my engineering college days ... second level of maturity, transition is little advanced here compared to school. Relationships goes through a phase of experiment where boys and girls trey to find many answers for confused questions like , is love real or we just find it in books and most of our Bollywood movies. How does it really feel to hide around the bushes and kiss each other ? Although the world is changing especially with the increasing popularity of western culture ... The kiss got promoted to making love; if things worked out, which was very rare. The second phase had gained so much popularity that it made its mark in our professional life too ... success, money, love, sex, party!

Fresh break-up - still this girl was so very normal. I was impressed and confused as well with both sides of her character. Impressed to see the normality she maintained after knowing the future of her relationship with Pratik. Did she really believe that serious relationships existed in this new era?

I said, "Well, I hope things get better. Now tell me what the good news is?"

She smiled, "Well, all of a sudden I got a call from Xeon Airlines for my final round of interview, so I had to rush to Mumbai and as an add-on, I met Pratik and he told me about his engagement the next month."

I was least interested about Pratik and asked, "And how was your interview?"

"Umm, it was okay" and with sheer excitement and energy in her voice she said, "And I got selected as cabin crew for Xeon Airlines. Yippy!"

Somehow this news made me happy too, "Wow Kaira! That's wonderful news! Congrats dear, very happy for you. So when is the treat?"

"Thank you so much, once I am back in Kolkata, then anytime you say?"

"Hold on, this means you are in Mumbai right now?"

"You dodo, check the number, it's Mumbai Vodafone," she laughed.

Yeah correct, I completely forgot, this is Mumbai Vodafone number. But why such a weird name for me?

I asked, "What is this dodo?"

"Hehehe, Dodo means dumb and it suits you, So from today onwards, I will call you dodo."

"Nonsense," I protested.

That hardly made any difference, because she kept laughing.

I asked, "This means you are in Mumbai now. So when are you going to come to Kolkata?"

"Good question dodo. In two weeks they are sending me to Gurgaon for a four-week training and after that I have no idea how the schedule will be."

That disappointed me, "Oh, so I won't get to meet you for quite some time then."

"*Kya baat hai*! Someone in Kolkata is dying to meet me," she teased.

"Shut up, do you need to find humour in everything and anything I say, always?"

"Ah, someone's getting angry now. Umm chill. I can imagine that you look very cute when you get angry."

All of a sudden I saw the bedside clock ... Shit! I have another fifteen minutes to get ready for office. I said, "Okay dearie, now I have a situation out here."

"What?"

"Talking to you, I forgot that I need to get ready for office. Now, have just less than fifteen minutes."

"Oh boy! I am so sorry, carry on! I forgot that you are a nocturnal human being," she said apologetically.

"Anything else?" I smiled.

"Have a good working day ahead and a vampire kiss on your neck. Bye."

"Bye dear and congrats once again."

"Thanks a ton."

"Welcome a million."

We laughed, said bye for one more time and disconnected the call.

I actually felt better after talking to her. The way she flirts, must say it's very impressive. May be the break up has something to do with her good mood. Anyway, her relationship was not heading anywhere. I prayed to God that she gets all the success she deserved in her new career.

My cell phone rang, "Hello."

"Sir, cab is waiting."

"I will be there in five minutes."

15

Truth 'N' Dare

I did tell Faiyaz the same day about Kaira and myself. He didn't utter a single word but only responded with his sometimes not so irritating smile.

Well, I won't waste time writing about this ninety percent affected mad guy Faiyaz Khan. For the last one week, there had been some interesting changes in my life, updates of which I would like to share. Sometimes there are a few things which you want to keep private but the temptation to resist certain things becomes very difficult.

After that night's conversation, Kaira and I kept in touch with each other, mostly voice conversations and for texting. Well, I had to go to the shop and add an unlimited sms pack (This gives a perfect picture of text message exchange between us throughout the day).

We started sharing our day to day activity. Initially I thought she was just kidding by calling me dodo but no, I was wrong. She actually made it a point to call me by that name diligently.

One Friday evening I got up a little early. To be honest, I set the alarm in my phone an hour-and-a-half before my wake-up time.

I called her up; she was surprised, "Dodo, what's wrong?"

I gently smiled and replied, "Nothing is wrong, why?"

Very bad acting, I realized. She said, "You need to work the whole night so now go and get some sleep for yourself."

Desperate counter-strike attempt from me, "Why, you don't want to talk?"

She softened her voice, "It's not that dodo. This is very bad, you are getting up early to talk to me, when you know you have to work the whole night."

"*Aaacha thik hai*, we will talk for some time and then I will go off to sleep again."

She took a deep breath, "Okay, but I won't fancy doing this again."

"Okay, deal. What are you up to?"

"Nothing much, watching TV."

"Where is aunty?"

"Mom went to the neighbour's flat to chit chat and you know dad usually comes back late."

I smiled, "See, I was sleeping and in my dream, I got a telepathic feeling that this is the right time to call you."

"Shut up, Dodo! *Kuch bhi haa?*"

I just laughed.

She said, "You know something?"

"What?"

"Has anyone ever told you that you are a completely mad person?"

I stopped laughing and replied, "No one has, but I'm aware of it."

Truth – n – Dare

Our chat session took a pretty serious turn suddenly for which neither of us was ready. It just happened.

After a few minutes of chit chat, we thought of playing truth and dare. We both were asking good/bad, sensible/insensible questions from each other.

I was asked, "What are the qualities you expect in your girl?"

I told her, "Mixture of good looks with a decent height and caring attitude."

Listening to my choice, she replied, "Not bad, dodo, but the combination is rare."

I tried flirting with her, "May be, may not be."

"What was that?"

"If no one else is there, then no worries ... *tum hoh na.*"

Seconds of silence and both of us laughed.

Next it was my turn to ask, "Will you ever get committed?"

"Umm I don't know. Let's see. If I get someone worth committing to, then why not?"

"Ahh, means Pratik was not worthy enough?"

"It's not about being worthy, dodo. I told you earlier ,remember, he is way older to me and we agreed mutually for a casual relationship so no major regrets from my end."

Truth and dare deviated to sensible discussion. We understood that but didn't interrupt each other.

"You know Kaira, here in Kolkata I've never heard or come across someone who is into such relationship but..." I was not able to complete my sentence, "And I am the first girl you came across with such experience, right?"

"Yeah, but listen I didn't mean you..."

"Chill, dodo, it's okay."

"Don't know Kaira but the more I talk to you, the more I get curious to know about you."

She smiled, "Really! Chalo then today you are free to ask me anything you want."

"Think again; I might ask you personal questions."

"Shoot."

I asked a straight forward question which was very spontaneous, "Are you a virgin?"

A moment of silence followed, I felt uneasy all of a sudden for asking such a bold question, which might get very embarrassing for a girl to answer.

I was about to apologize. Kaira didn't let me do that, "No, I am not."

"I am terribly sorry Kaira. I know it is a very personal thing to ask."

"No need to apologize, dodo, and please don't keep saying sorry and make our friendship look so formal."

I was numb. In a little high pitch she asked, "Now what's wrong with you?"

In a very soft tone, I replied, "Nothing."

"See dodo, I don't feel bad for what I did, just enjoyed and lived those moments. In fact, if I ever hook up with any guy, I will definitely tell him the truth about my past. Now you must be thinking what a weird type of girl I am, right?"

"Not at all, Kaira. In fact, I respect your bold attitude and courage to speak the truth."

"Hmm," I heard the sound of the door bell from the other end of the line.

Kaira said, "Aachcha dodo, guess mom is here. You take rest, will talk to you later."

"Okay dear, bye."

"Bye."

The intense energy to live life to the fullest with her inspired me somewhere. She was right with her thought and it made sense-if you have to accept someone in your life, then that person has to be accepted with his/her packages. Actually it's very easy to lie about something, but you need to be fearless to speak the truth. Not fake but real smile started to unravel on my face. I don't know when, but unknowingly, the house of broken emotions started rebuilding itself. The thought of Anushka still remained in my mind, though just like a harmless photograph. Initially I used to think why she lied to me all along with all the drama? Was it to make me feel miserable? I must say it did make me feel so for some time but the entire thing depended on my personal choice. And today, I've found happiness.

A memorable evening

A week had already passed by and we had been over the phone for almost ten hours a day, phew! Sorry, wow! Incredible it is!

After the abrupt ending of the truth and dare game, never again did we raise those topics. The best part was, it did not affect our friendship at all, but it did affect my feelings towards her with a deeper sense of understanding.

The excitement of joining work on the first day has always been more exciting than getting a job. Don't know about others but my first working day in Wipro will always be the most memorable day of my life. So I can understand the level of excitement through which Kaira was passing from within, with just another leftover four days and couple of breathtaking hours before she joined Xeon Airlines.

Four weeks of training in Delhi and after that, no idea when I would get to meet her. It would have been perfect if her hiring airlines could have organized the same training at Dumdum International Airport.

I tend to forget that the Software and Aviation industry are two completely different fields. I told myself, "Get used to it Mr. Aryan Roy; there are plenty of unknown things coming your way."

I was in office and fortunately there wasn't much work which fell under the exception list. Bad luck for Faiyaz Khan that he got stuck with the same shitty client call. I sat in my cubicle all jobless, my cell phone vibrated-text message flashed up on the mobile screen –

Kaira : *"What's up, dodo?"*

Aryan : *"No fans, just seeing a blank white ceiling with flashy white lights, lolz!"*

Kaira : *"Just shut up! Stop cracking your bad PJ. What you doing?"*

Aryan : *"Jobless at office, just sitting idle, btw what you doing so late? Missing me, huh?"*

Kaira : *"Yeah I am actually missing you, felt like, so texted you."*

Aryan : *"Are you serious?"*

Kaira : *"Why? Do you find anything abnormal in this?"*

Aryan : *"Nehi shona, just asking like that."*

Kaira : *"Dodo..."*

Aryan : *"Yeah baby."*

Instant, a reply came which was more surprising than what I imagined.

Kaira : *"Muaaaahhhhhhzzz."*

WTF! Did she just send me a kiss. No way, wow! I mean, I didn't know how to respond; was thinking what to reply but before that just then, text popped up on the screen.

Kaira : *"Don't know dodo jus felt like giving you a kissi."*

Aryan : *"I so feel like going and giving you a tight little hug."*

Kaira : *"Awwwwwieee cho chweet."*

Aryan : ☺

I was so engrossed in my text chat that I didn't realize Faiyaz standing right behind me. I looked at him and as always, hesaid with a gentle smile, "Mr. Jobless, if your romancing is done, can we go for a smoke?"

I objected, "I am not romancing for a your kind inforimation."

"*Accha thik hai,* don't have to tell me. *Abhi chaal yaar.*"

We came out of the cubicle stretch to the lobby and headed towards the smoking zone, I asked him while we were walking, "How did the call go?"

"Nothing new, the discussions just went round and round in circles and landed up at the same place."

Cellphone beeped - Kaira : *"Me feeling sleepy dodo, what time will you log out?"*

Aryan : *"Still a long day ahead of me,just came out with Faiyaz for a smoke. You go and take rest, will log off and call you. Good night Chocó drmzzz☺"*

Kaira : *"Oki Toki dodo and say hi to Faiyaz. Hope hez doing gud. Bye"*

Aryan : *"Bye bye dear, sleep tight."*

I kept the cell phone inside my pocket and told Faiyaz, "Kaira said hi to you."

He did not reply and we entered the smoking zone silently. He lit a cigarette and leaving one ring of smoke said, "Wanted to ask you something."

"What?"

"*Kya chal raha hai* between you and Kaira?"

I saw this coming, "Nothing as such. We're just friends." I released one ring of smoke from my mouth.

"I've been noticing your behaviour for the past couple of days and it seems you're lost in some other world."

"Why? Am I acting weird?"

"Sort of."

I walked up to him and showed him our little conversation. After reading it he patted my back, "Good going Romeo, that means you've crossed the 'just friends' phase."

I snatched the cellphone from his hand, "I really can't tell what's going on between us."

"I hope it turns out to be love."

"Dude listen, I will catch up with you in the cafeteria in another hour. Aniket has called me. Enjoy your cigarette." He walked out of the smoking zone. I was still there to finish my leftover cigarette.

The office campus looked beautiful after dawn – three huge buildings enclosing our more than amazing three storeyed glass cafeteria. I still remember, when I was in school, looking at the campus from outside, I used to think that it was one of the building where employees worked, but to my surprise it turned out to be a food-joint for employees with multiple food vendors.

This much was clear that Kaira liked me and so did I. Now the million dollar question was – should I express my feelings to her or directly talk to her and clear my confusion? Should I do this before she left for Delhi or wait for her to meet up me. Faiyaz advised to go ahead. In a way, he wasn't wrong. So much of planning with Anushka and the end result was a disaster. In that case there was no harm in taking a serious try with Kaira. I understand she belonged to a different culture and profession which might turn out to be less challenging, but not to worry as long as the effort was two-sided.

16

A two-kilometre stretch of road to my house was in a complete mess due to drainage system work which was going on and made my life miserable, sort of. We all knew the pace of development in our country (all thanks to our politicians) and if we talked about Kolkata, patience was the only thing that we all needed to work towards. Working at night was all about getting adapted to the time change but returning thirty-two kilometres home in bright sunlight crossing all major signals of Kolkata got very tiring. The drainage construction on the main road was an added torture.

After freshening up, I texted Kaira.

Aryan : *"Baby, feeling very tired. I will get up and call you."*

Instant reply – Kaira : *"Vampire kiss on your neck."*

I got up and checked the bed-clock; it was 11.20 p.m., still had another hour to sleep. I took out the cell phone and dialled her known number.

"Hello, dodo."

"What are you doing?"

"I'm packing up stuff for my training. But the sound of your voice is so tempting," she said, adding some passion to her voice.

"Trust me, the world should learn the art of flirting from you."

She laughed, "Oh, thank you dodo, I am honoured."

I just smiled. She asked, "Do you wish to fall back to sleep?"

"I so wish to do that and see you in my dreams."

"Now who's flirting?"

"What do I do? It's your effect on me."

"F*** you!!!"

With a bit of energy in my voice, I said "I'd love it!!"

Her sweet-angry voice revolted, "Oh god! You are impossible, dodo."

I just laughed and in that course, my sleepiness got reduced to a large extent.

We kept on pulling each other's leg until I said I had to go and freshen up.

"Oh sure, it's about time. You are stinking; you need it bad!"

I smiled and asked, "When will you go off to sleep?"

"When you board the cab, call me. If I am awake, will talk."

"Okay, but I have a question."

"What?"

"How will you F*** me if I am in Kolkata and you in Delhi?"

"You are pathetic."

"He he. I know. Bye."

"Bye."

I had already started feeling fresh with such a semi-hot conversation. Was it love or something else, I do not know, but what made it all worthwhile was that we both clicked really well. She made me happy.

I was hoping maybe I could talk things out with Faiyaz. This bloke, although he acted funny and less serious most of the time, when it comes to legit talks, he was the one person who could come up with really mature and good advices. He was the real deal.

The cab was on time; I got inside and dialed her number. No response; re-dialed, no response again.

I was in no mood to work then on and the good news was that there was no work. I asked Faiyaz if he could come down to the tea stall and he was there.

I told him all the encounters I had with Kaira and the least he could reply me with after everything was just, "Hmmm."

"Oye! What Hmmm?? Tell me something yaar."

A long sip of tea, he responded "Thinking."

"Now what the hell are you thinking?"

"Thinking about whatever's going on in my mind, shall I tell you?"

"Stop creating confusion now; tell me."

"*Dekh bhai,* I think you should propose to her. Based on what you said, it seems both of you are going along pretty smoothly and the main thing is there is no harm in giving it a try, right? If things don't work out, then remain good friends."

"Are you sure?"

"Yes, I am. But you need to adjust yourself a lot. Firstly she is not a Bengali, secondly she is from Mumbai and lastly apart from cultural differences, it's long distance."

"I agree and to add on, her profession is complete opposite to mine."

"So what do you want to do?"

"I think, I should go ahead … you are right, there is no harm in trying."

"I just noticed one thing about her, not sure if you will like it."

Typical Faiyaz, unbeatable in keeping an uninvited question mark glowing above your head anytime. Surprised, I asked, "What did you notice?"

"I could be wrong, but I feel she is too easy going and casual in life, which might be a problem in the future at some point."

I kept quiet, trying to figure out what he had just said. I decided. No point, it's no jackpot game I am playing. I am going for it.

Looked at my phone's digital watch and our login time passed way back; I prayed that Aniket be in a good mood lest the opening ceremony of work would definitely be half-an-hour or longer awareness session about the seriousness and dedication needed at the workplace.

17

The final judgment!

One more night to go and Kaira was moving to Delhi for almost a month. We had a word the night before last and she seemed to be very excited for her job.

Mentally I decided to say I loved her; made several attempts to reveal that but all in vain. Didn't know but something was pulling me was back, could be anything – fear of rejection which might hurt my dignity or is it the fear of losing her as a good friend? She was a friend of Anushka and I was not sure whether Kaira was in touch with her. I was extremely grateful to her for whatever she had done but if I express my feelings towards her, there was a chance that she might think otherwise, that I had been trying to take advantage of her sensitive emotions.

Damn! Whoever said love is not complicated, must've been a saint. It's not only complicated but it's like taking a spaceship and entering a black hole where entry and exit are both equally uncertain to a large extent.

The thought of Anushka being in touch with Kaira created a sudden burning sensation within me. Let her know that I am dating her best friend, I didn't care what the consequences would be; today I would express my feelings. She should not be my reason for being sad; she should be my reason of success in introducing me to her best friend. The show began.

I skipped office. Aniket was busy giving me lectures about the business impact if I missed a day but I didn't care. Somehow I felt that these types of creatures should not have girlfriends, and marriage is an absolute no. Firstly, if they were ordered to stay at work for sixteen hours a day anytime, in spite of not being single, they would blindly agree to it (to hell with family, precisely). Secondly, they strictly follow the mantra of 'never say no to boss(es).' And lastly, they always give very diplomatic answers. To be truthful, I categorize them as a bunch of losers who lack entertainment in their life.

Mission impossible ahead: I got up early evening and called up Kaira. As I heard the phone ringing, my heart beat accelerated mildly.

"Dodo, why are you up so early?"

"I'm off from work, so yeah."

"Why?"

"I decided not to look at the office cubicle today."

"Not a convincing answer, she said in s sing-song tone."

I was quiet. In fact, there was seriousness in my voice which called for her attention. She asked, "What's wrong, dodo?"

Gently I replied, "Nothing at all."

She was not convinced, "Very well, are you sure, though? Cause I can sense that something is not right at your end."

I tried changing the topic, "So you're done with all your packing?"

Some unexpected light bashing followed, "Listen, to hell with packing, now don't force me to be rude to you and tell me what's going on."

I took a deep breath, "Kaira, I'm starting to have a deep feeling for you, I think I'm in love ... with you."

"What?"

Her response made me nervous, "Look, I know this sounds weird but I mean..." I started stammering.

She laughed her lungs out; I felt very embarrassed. Getting stuck in such an awkward situation, I was absolutely numb with repeated desperate attempts to find words.

She stopped laughing, "Dodo, you love me?"

My stammering continued "Yes, I mean ... no…"

"What, okay so you don't love me?"

I controlled myself at least tried my best, "Yes, I do."

"Muaaaahhhhhhzzz! I knew this was coming from you, but didn't expect it so early."

"I thought I will wait till you return from Delhi, but somehow failed to suppress my feelings."

"But before I give you any answer, Dodo, you know my past, I mean about my past relationship."

"Yes, I do."

"Whatever I've been through, you know there's no regret and in my current relation, I don't wish for my guy to dwell in my past."

"Kaira, honestly I don't care what you've done in the past but I do care of what you do in your present and your future, so you can count on me for that."

"Are you sure?"

"Yes, I am, but I fear something,"

"What?"

"Our relation can spoil your friendship with Anushka and I get a guilt feeling thinking about that."

"Don't be, dodo. I will handle that. It's her bad luck that she failed to understand you."

I did not reply, rather just gave a gentle smile.

She smiled and continued, "You know something dodo, the first impression I had of you wasn't all that great."

"Really?"

"Yes, I felt you were very introvert but gradually you showed the real picture."

"And what is that?"

"Creative, emotional, jovial and a simple heart. Now don't start flying okay?"

"I won't, but you still did not give any answer to my question."

"Dumb, you still need an answer?"

"Yes."

"Yes, dodo, I love you too."

"Umm..."

"Shut up."

Seconds of silence later laughter got exchanged at both ends of the line.

It was one of the best evenings of my life. Sounds much like some typical Bollywood love story. I went to meet the girl I was after for so many years and currently dating her best friend, to add-on, she was the one who introduced me to this girl. The thought of Anushkha getting furious after hearing about Aryan-Kaira affair gave me a deep internal satisfaction.

Finally, I got a girl for whom I can proudly say, she's the girl I love.

Kaira promised me, after going to Delhi for training she would be in constant touch with me and once the training was over, based on the situation we would then meet up. I thanked God for showering me with happiness after all the frustrations I had gone through.

Listening to everything, Faiyaz gave me mixed expressions. His comment, "Dude, I said this earlier too but again your choice and confidence is what matters the most. See, I am not saying that she is not a good girl, but due to cultural differences plus long distance being a big milestone, it's something both of you need to work on and put a lot of effort in. Right now, I will just sit and watch how you handle her."

This raised a question, "What do you mean by, 'how you handle her'?"

"Like I've said before, she seems to be a really easy going person and you'll have to compromise, sacrifice and put in a lot for you to get used to her."

"Yeah, all the best to me."

"All the best, bhai."

External sites cannot be opened on our office computer but who cares. We are twenty first century Indians, the land of software gurus. The solution to this problem is simple, change the proxy settings of the computer. I saw the Orkut login screen. I changed my relationship status from 'Single' to 'Committed'.

18

One week update

Kaira's airline training was at its peak. I got to know a lot of things about this unknown profession – grooming sessions for proper hairstyle and makeup, formal dress code, mandatory swimming training, midnight training at airport about job roles of the cabin crew, learning about crucial aircraft parts and so on. Another day I was talking to her and came to know a good thing; we all travel on planes and before take-off we see one of the members of the crew closing the aircraft door. Kaira and other trainees in her batch went through one full day's training just to learn how to close and open the door properly. During duty if they fail to perform this operation even with slight mistake, it's a straight termination. Sounds very weird, but that's the truth.

The fifth day of her training was Saturday and Sundays are break days for her, so she planned to go to a night club along with four other girls. Hearing this, I objected and landed up into a small telephonic fight with her.

"Is it really necessary for you to go?"

"Dodo, everyone is going – now if I stay back I will get bored. Please dodo, please please please," she continued.

"Kaira, you're not understanding, Delhi is not safe for girls, especially at night."

"Chill dodo, I told you about my roommate Smita, remember?"

"Yes."

"Two of her friends are coming in .They are co-pilots of our airlines and locals in Delhi. So don't worry."

"One condition..."

"What?"

"Once you're home, make sure you intimate me."

"Muahhh, okay honey I will do, and cheer up now."

"You take care, I will go and get ready now."

Once again, I got convinced. I go clubbing with my friends sometimes, but I know that the nightlife in Kolkata and Mumbai in that sense is safe; Delhi on the other hand is different. It does not hve a good reputation when it comes to that as per the news. There is no harm if my girlfriend goes out clubbing, but don't know why I got so possessive about her. It reminded me of what Faiyaz had said about compromising and adjusting to the current situation.

Saturday night, Faiyaz and gang planned to do something else and after getting to know the plan, I too said yes instantly. We drove down to Sher-e-Punjab Dhaba near Kolaghat for a late night dinner.

Everything said and done, a fire inside my heart kept me restless the whole night because I was basically waiting for her to get back to me. On the way to the Dhaba, I tried calling her once, but her phone was out of range.

I reached back home at around 4.30 a.m., yet no call or text from Kaira. I tried calling her and this time it was switched off. To make things even worse, I didn't have any of her friend's, number. The dinner was good but somehow my mind was somewhere else and it's very annoying when shit like this happens. She should have called me. I was lying on the bed without any sleep; after every minute, I would look at my cell phone, but I wasn't luck.

I waited and waited, but I couldn't remember when I closed my eyes to sleep. The cell phone was on loud and vibrating mode, it started ringing all of a sudden. I was too drowsy to even check who was calling.

"Hi, Dodo."

My sleep vanished in a flash of seconds, "Where the hell were you the whole night?"

She started stammering, "I am sorry dodo, I was sloshed yesterday. I somehow managed to come back home but was in no condition of even lift my cell phone."

I raised my voice then, "Do you have any idea, I was not able to sleep the whole night worrying about you."

"Dodo, I am so sorry. I'll make sure that such thing won't happen in the future. Please give me a smile, muaaahhh, please."

"Kaira grow up, I don't mind if you go out clubbing, but you can't be so irresponsible."

"Honey, I said sorry. Now please cheer up, this will never happen again."

I really don't know why I always got convinced by her; this is wrong. Was it because of her confidence or her convincing nature? That was the last chance I decided to give and hoped she would keep her promise.

19

Thoughts flowing

Kaira went for clubbing a few more times after the first mishap, but she made sure she kept her words. On another note, it was sort of like a thing for me to tackle her out of her drunken state of mind. Alcohol makes us do or say things we never intend to when we're sober.

Before I go further ahead with this story, I would like to confess one thing: The drunken Kaira sounded way better than the normal Kaira. I am not saying that normally she is not good, but there is something different when she is drunk – mind speaks freely, sounds raunchy and naughty (Wish I was physically present in front of her); it increases the desire within me to meet her right at that moment while in real life it wasn't possible. No worries, a time will come for me to get sloshed along with her, I consoled myself.

As of late, the only thought which created an itch in my heart was Anushka. I was sure she has checked my relationship status on my Orkut profile. I was not sure if Kaira had any contact with her and had told her about our relationship. If she had been updated with the current changes in my life, then why were there no reactions till now? I had been after a girl madly since my school days but she never acknowledged my feelings and then one fine day I meet her friend, don't know if it was a coincidence or destiny that when she was on the verge of breaking-up with me, I instead hooked up with the friend. In the beginning, when my relationship was shaping up with Kaira, I used to stay confused, wondering if I could ever get over a girl whom I had been after since high school? Does it mean my current relationship was just a medium of taking revenge from Anushka? A couple of times I asked myself these questions. I knew this relationship took shope earlier than expected but I loved Kaira. And to be honest, I was not here to play any game in which she had to be made a puppet.

Destination – Digha

The weekend was approaching again and having heard about my promotion in personal life, Faiyaz and the gang decided to go to "Digha" to celebrate. It's a Bay of Bengal surrounded tourist area with nothing different compared to any other beach-attached small town.

Couples go there for romantic weekends and honeymoons; and it's the same place they have probably been to numerous times with family, friends or maybe with the same boy/girl they are married to.

On asking them, "How was your honeymoon?" Happily they will reply, "It was very romantic Aryan; the fish cooked on the beach was yummy"

Going to the seaside and a Bengali not talking about fish will be a rare exception.

On Friday, there was not much of work in office and all my friends – Faiyaz, Indrajeet, Sunny – had come with their travelling bags. The plan was to clock out from office, go to Esplanade and board a bus from there to Digha.

When I entered the office, Indrajeet was the first person I met. Looking at me he literally shouted, "*Aare dada,* congratulations!"

His level of excitement and pitch of voice was abnormally high; I looked around and noticed a couple of other colleagues of staring at us, trying to figure out what was going on.

I went near Indra and said, "Control your voice, ass; we don't have to make it public."

He stuck out his tongue and said, "So sorry boss, it was out of excitement .When Faiyaz told me about the Digha plan and the reason of celebration, I instantly said yes. Anyway show me the photo."

"I shall show it to you during the break, I said."

"At Digha, we are going to rip you off, man."

"You are threatening me already..."

"Why would I threaten you, boss? Want to hear the entire story of where, when, how? And then we will drink till my stomach is full with beer."

Faiyaz Khan arrived in the meanwhile. Keeping one hand on my shoulder, he asked, "What's up, Romeo?"

I was not able to control my laughter, but somehow stopped and said, "*Kuch bhi,* huh?"

"Why, am I wrong?"

"There's no point talking to you on this."

"Very good, I like your faith in me. Now let's go and have a cigarette, I am already feeling the deficiency of nicotine in my blood."

"How can you talk shit with such consistency?"

"God gifted for special persons on earth. Now, let's go."

I could already tell how the whole trip was going to be. Indra already gave me a minor hint of some teasing around and above all, four drunken boys together, I am sure everyone could guess the consequences. After the shift, it would be "*Mission Digha.*"

Like other Bengalis, even I have been to this place numerous times with my parents and really have some good memories of my early school days. The place used to be less crowded and staying at my dad's company's guest house called "Ranshwik House" was a delight. It was named after the first British resident of Digha on a hilltop with a beautiful view of the Bay of Bengal – massive wooden British styled antique bun glow with a garden on every side along with the huge runway for Sir Ranshwik's plane.

There were no phone calls or text from Kaira, her in-flight training had started and she intimated me the day before about the hectic day ahead. It's really a strange module of training these airline people follow – in-flight training from 11 PM. We IT employees say "On the job training is like honeymoon period" and coming back to aviation, the rule changes upside down. I looked at the time, another three hours of training were left for her. No point calling her now, it would be switched off anyway.

Early next morning, I received a text from Kaira, "Very tired Dodo, will hit the bed and maybe speak to you tomorrow." My heart commanded me to go ahead and give her a call but mind stopped me my. I replied, "No problem baby, sleep tight ... i'll reach and call you in the evening. Love you."

Thank god I am not in Xeon, God bless Wipro (lolz!).

20

The journey!

After office, we were in no hurry to catch the bus for Digha. We first reached Esplanade and entered one cheap. It was already too hot in Kolkata with the sun ready to kiss our faces, so we mutually decided to overcome dehydration with some chilled beer.

The journey was pleasant, no major events; everyone slept like a baby after the graveyard shift.

The bus halted for lunch in some Dhaba, none of us got down though. Sitting on my seat, half asleep, I dialled Kaira as number. Within a minutes, she responded, "Hello Dodo."

"Hi honey, what you doing?"

Indrajeet was sitting beside me and upon hearing the word "Honey" he gave me a wicked smile and closed his eyes again. That explained everything on how my boys would not miss a chance to tease me.

Kaira replied, "Just got done showering."

"Umm, you smell delicious."

"I know, righttt!" after giving a small laugh, she asked, "What about you?"

"Still on the way dear; should reach in the next two hours, I guess."

"So, ready for a blast?"

"You can say so."

"Accha listen, I am going out clubbing today."

This changed my mood in a fraction of seconds. I asked, "Again?"

I sensed sort of a revolt in her voice "What do you mean by again? Even you are going out on a trip with your friends."

My stretching it would mean a massive brawl, so I voiced down a bit, "Not like that baby, just asking, have fun and keep in touch."

I succeeded and failed to an extent to move out of this topic. With an irritating tone, she said, "Oh god! Aryan, I will be fine and can take care of myself, so stop worrying and you too chill out today."

"I didn't get you."

"What I mean is, let's take a break today. You have fun with your friends and so will I."

Not so convinced, I replied, "Oh like that."

"Yes like that, honey."

"Okay, dear."

"Chalo, I will hang up now; feeling cold."

"Why, you aren't wearing anything?"

" Haha, you nasty. I rushed out of the shower wrapped in a towel the moment I heard my phone ringing."

I laughed.

"Okay, now bye dodo. Enjoy your trip ana have a blast."

"You too have fun and stay safe. Bye."

I couldn't really decide if I should be upset or happy about that, but never mind, it was all good. Loads of events awaited and if I passed on the current conversation details to Faiyaz, then I was sure that he would take a royal class right away. So better I didn't say anything.

Beer, Bonfire and Brainless Conversations

By the time we reached, it was burning hot in Digha and taking a dip in the sea was beyond question. Sunny knew a hotel and rooms were pre-booked by him from Kolkata itself so we checked in, filled our hungry stomach with the great seafood meal and lastly, we got to have a sensation of cold water under the shower.

There was a big lawn in front of the hotel, sea-facing. We all decided to party on the lawn rather than going for a walk down the beach.

Fifteen bottles of beer were our companion with bon fire. And that's when the interrogation session started.

Indrajeet was holding a bottle and asked me, "Aachcha now tell ... tell me how, how everything happened?"

I looked far ahead, embraced the beauty of it all voluptuously and ignored him.

Faiyaz voiced out, "Indra, see he is already blushing. Now it has happened na, so how, why, when does not matter."

"My curiosity was aroused when you told me that Aryans is dating an air-hostess. I, for a fact, would love to know how it all happened."

I broke my silence finally, "Well, she happened to be my best friend's really good friend. After my break up, we developed feelings for each other. So that's how it all started."

He looked up to count the stars maybe, and then looked at me, "Boss, keep your love story to yourself. You got me confused right in the beginning."

Everyone laughed aloud; Faiyaz came near me and whispered, "Saved your ass today from getting raped, you owe me a beer in Kolkata."

I just replied, "Sure thing, deal."

The first guy to get sloshed was Sunny. He has a very bad habit of kissing people's, cheeks in a very irritating way whenever liquor got heavy on him. Faiyaz and I were aware of this activity, so before he could enact his nonsense, both of us moved away from him. Sadly Indrajeet was his prey this time. Before poor Indra could understand anything, Sunny went near him and suddenly gave a tight kiss on his left cheek. Indra pushed him away and shouted, "Get lost, you bloody homo..."

Sunny did not answer, but gave a wicked smile.

I was sitting beside Faiyaz; looking at this funny scene. We could not control our laughter; falling on his lap, bottle in hand and one hand on my stomach, I bursted out.

Somehow I managed to stop my laughter and told Sunny, "Oye, he just said you are a homo. Is that true?"

Calmly, Sunny replied, "He is backdated Aryan bhai, can't help."

Laughter burst out again. Indra was sitting and staring at us; his eyes were on fire.

I thanked Kaira within my mind, for the development of our relationship. Faiyaz had planned everything and it turned out to be such a super chilled evening. From the thought of Kaira, I scrolled through the call-list in my cellphone to dial her number, but recapitulated what we had agreed on – no calls, just chill out with our respective groups. I put my cellphone back into my pocket.

Indra stood up suddenly and raising the beer bottle with his right hand said, "Okay everyone, the reason we came here for – a toast for Aryan and Kaira." Sunny and Faiyaz raised their bottles too.

I just said, "Thank you guys, thank you very much."

I must say, life is really so unpredictable. Look at my life as an example – a couple of months ago, I was sitting in Gariahat, confused and clueless about the future of my personal life. And fast forward it to today: I am sitting here in front of the massive Bay of Bengal, enjoying the moment of celebration organized by my friends for getting a promotion from being single to committed.

We decided that in the morning we would take a bath in the sea and in the afternoon, head back for Kolkata. The last bottle really gave me a kick. It was time to grab some sleep and get up early for the sunrise the next day.

While walking towards the room, once again the hidden itching thought struck: Is Anushka aware of this entire thing? Or is she just not bothered enough to express her anger because of her ego? Somehow I managed to push the thought away from my already short-circuited mind.

21

Being an Indian

Next day, we come back to Kolkata and in hell, my workplace. It's a real tough job, focusing on work after you come back from a refreshing holiday and it's even more irritating when your boss gives you a lecture about your performance and European bosses are not happy with your performance. In fact, I should say that sucks big time. They should actually look into the market reality of what our Indian employees are capable of. It's true and unfair that our managers sitting in India don't respect the efforts everyone have put to achieve this milestone.

A couple of years back, when the entire world was struggling to survive the economic slowdown, in spite of the numerous cows on the Indian roads, we sold the maximum numbers of Mercedes, Audis and BMWs along with the Marutis and Tatas. Indian banks sustained a reasonable fall but remained considerably stable while the big bosses started filing for bankrupty. The retail industry boomed in India more than any other country.

Just like Dr. Shashi Tharoor said in his "The elephant, the tiger and the cell phone" that we now have 500 million or more cell phone users which make us larger than the U.S. The users come from every nook and corner of the country, irrespective of their financial capability. Apart from the metropolitan cities, even people in small towns prefer to have an iPhone or a BlackBerry rather than any other regular devices.

Looking at all these true facts from where I was born, I guess it's a shame that our managers are unaware of all these details. Again just a reminder to all readers , that it is just my frustration coming out after getting back to work from an eventful holiday.

Kaira calling Aryan

It was early in the morning when we all gathered to sit and chat over coffee in the cafeteria. Kaira called. I looked at Faiyaz and got up from my seat, "Hey baby!"

"Hi Dodo, how are you?"

"I am good dearie, what about you?"

"I am doing well."

Her voice was sounding pretty low, I asked, "So how was your training?"

"Fortunately, it got cancelled."

I came out of the cafeteria to the lawn, "Why are you sounding so low?"

"Nothing honey, I partied too hard last night. I puked and now am struggling with a bad hangover."

I know one thing for sure by now, giving any type of suggestions to her with regards to this partying stuff will only land us into a brawl. So I asked her diplomatically, "Did you take any medicines?"

"Yes, I did. Feeling much better now, though."

"Good," was the only word I could come up with.

"Now you tell me dodo, how was your trip?"

I walked down from the lawn to the main gate for a smoke while talking, "The trip was awesome, enjoyed every bit of it and got drunk but no hangover luckily."

"Did you take loads of pictures?"

"Took a couple of them, will mail them to you this coming weekend."

"Dodo, I am feeling very nervous."

"Why, what's the matter?"

"Training is about to get over and most probably, by next month, they'll be allotting us flights to operater."

"Well, that's what you're there for; you'll eventually have to go through it sooner or later, so without losing confidence, put in your best effort."

"I'm impressed with how much faith and confidence you have in me."

"It's my duty to support and build up your confidence as your boyfriend."

"Muahhh."

"Don't distract me; I am in office."

"You're a pro at multi-tasking, so I shouldn't worry about a thing," she laughed.

I laughed and replied, "What a neat comeback."

"Bakwaas!"

I laughed.

A thought came to my mind to visit her in Delhi in case we don't get to meet often, especially once she started with work there's very litle possibility that she would get to take some time off from work. Even if she did, heaven knows how she'd decide to make use of it. Moreover, the chance was high that she does not get Kolkata layovers. Right after that thought, another one hit me, that Anushka too lived in Delhi so the former thought went right away. I for once did not wish to breath the same air that she breathes, to be close to something that would remind me of her.

It's amazing how time changed everything. For a minute I was head over heels in love with her, things were so close to perfect, and the next minute, all of the love, time and thoughts spent amounted to nothing.

I went back to the cafeteria. As I sat down Faiyaz asked, "Everything all right?"

I replied, "Yes dude, rocking!"

He patted my shoulder and said, "Shabash, my tiger!"

22

An Unexpected Call

For the last few days, the telephonic tête-à-tête between me and Kaira had trimmed down. We had become busy. Her training phase was now over, time for her to fly back. The crew who were in the same flight for two weeks travelling across India got accustomed to their role and to each other. In between all this, she tried to keep in touch through text notes and brief communications every now and then.

Again came another awaited weekend, not a zilch had been planned yet. I was at home with a sense of laziness to tread out of the house; sometimes it happens to many of us, when on that one day, we just love squandering some quality time on ourselves. Above all, our parents have a propensity to be happy seeing their children at home on a Saturday, a rare episode. That very day, dad was both in high spirits and surprised, which led me to an unusual satisfaction seeing him smile.

Faiyaz had gone out on a date with a girl from the workplace, she being an unfamiliar face gave me an opportunity for this anticipated break. I was relishing my fine taste in socio-political non-fiction books. I decided to spend that evening with the book *The five dollar smile.*

I was just about completely occupied with the exquisite narrative from the book named *The Village Girl,* when my cell phone started to ring.

I felt disgusted, "Why the f*** was she calling me?"

I stared at my phone for a good long minute. I was lost somewhere until I realized it had stopped ringing. My brainpower was in a perplexed state; what was I suppose to do? Like a bolt from the blue, the phone started ringing again.

I answered, "Hello."

"Hi Aryan, how are you?"

I kept my voice as normal as possible, "Hey Anushka! What a pleasant surprise! I am good dear, what about you?"

"Doing good, Aryan. So what are you doing?"

"Nothing much, I am at home, reading."

She smiled, "That's surprising."

"Well, you can say so."

"By the way listen, are you free now?"

"Yes, kind of."

"Can you meet up now, it's kind of critical."

I was still in a state of trance; I asked "What? Now? You are in Kolkata?"

"Yes, I got here this afternoon."

"Is everything alright?"

"Yes, I mean no. Well, can you meet me?"

I looked at the wall clock, it was already eight. I asked, "It's late, is it okay with you?"

"I wouldn't be asking if I wasn't okay with it now, would I?"

I was quiet, still confused about what to say. She repeated in a heavy voice, "Are you listening to me?"

"Yeah, okay where shall I come?"

"You tell me."

I thought for a minute, tried really hard to think of all the places to go at this time of the evening and replied, "Why don't you suggest the place?"

I could sense the irritation in her voice, "Okay, are you driving down?"

"Yes, I have to. This is not a very handy time to chase public transport, after all."

"Indeed, please pick me up on your way; let's go for a drive."

"Okay! See you by nine?"

Here I lost a night to stay at home and have some family bonding. My contemplation that dad would have been happy to have all of us home during a weekend. For a moment I thought if I should call up Kaira and talk to her about this sudden visit of Anushka? My conscience so I let it be.

While I was grabbing the car keys on the way out, dad asked why I was going to take the car out and how absurd it was for a Saturday evening. I replied, "Urgent situation of a friend, dad. I will be back before you even know that I'm gone."

Most irritating drive of my life

While driving down towards Jadavpur, the reiterated events of the past flashed back like a clipped movie, which irritated me. Why did I take her call? Why did I not misbehave? What was she doing in Kolkata all of a sudden? And lastly, why was she so frantic to meet me? Driving and trying to find answers to all these questions further intrigued me. Was she aware that I was in a relationship with her school companion? If she was, is her visit to Kolkata related to it? God! I would go crazy. Felt like pounding my head on the steering wheel. What a slow moving traffic even on a Saturday! I made my way through the traffic, overtaking and making my way. I could hear the curses from several auto-rickshaws and other cars. I finally reached Jadavpur 8B bus stop on time.

"Hello Anushka, I am waiting downstairs, in front of your apartment."

"Give me five minutes Aryan; I will be there."

Although there were no grounds to be so, but I was extremely nervous. More than Anushka, Even because I was apprehensive about how Kaira would react when she will come to know from me about all this? Till now, I had not hidden anything from her and once I went back home today, I would tell her everything.

In less than five minutes, Anushka was standing in front of me. I hugged her and asked, "What are you on about? Is everything fine at home?"

She looked at me, gave an insipid smile and replied, "Yes, don't worry, things are fine at home."

"Then, all of a sudden why are you in Kolkata?"

"Surprised?"

"Don't you think that's acceptable?"

"It is, get into the car."

While opening the car door, I could clearly see thousands of smouldering question marks on my forehead; no point in enacting Mr. Sherlock Holmes now. These unknowns can only be answered by the one sitting beside me.

I asked, "So where are we going?"

"Highland Park."

"Okay" I started the car, reversed and drove out.

I was quiet, strange it was; the girl with whom I used to talk for hours was sitting right beside me and I tried my level best to think of something to talk about.

Anushka broke the silence, "Had your dinner?"

Listening to this, my humour faded and I asked rudely, "Did you call me from so far off to ask what I had for dinner?"

"Why are you getting so hyped up?"

I did not answer; just looked at the windshield and concentrated on driving.

Now with a commanding and heavy tone she said, "I wanted to say something very important."

I looked at her, "Is there anything important left between us to discuss about?" I looked at the windshield again.

She got furious this time and shouted, "Mr. Aryan Roy, can you please pack your anger for some time and listen to me?"

I took a right from EM Bypass towards the Highland Park, just half a kilometre away from destination.

I tried my level best to control my anger and politely asked, "First tell me, what you are you doing in Kolkata so suddenly?"

"I came for you, idiot."

Bloody hell! This answer was unexpected, "What?"

"Yes, and I know many things are going on inside your head; the voices in your head are questioning your conscience. But park the car and then we can talk."

The unbearable truth came out

After parking the car, we got out and sat outside the shopping mall. Although it was late evening, and it being a Saturday, there was a good chunk of crowd around us. Moreover, the newspaper had advertised a hefty discount on shopping at Highland Park shopping mall.

Anushka was sitting beside me; I said, "Now tell me."

"Okay but first promise me, you won't freak out."

I kept quiet for some time and said, "Depends on what you are going to say."

"Please Aryan, just one last time, I can only request you."

"Fine."

"You and Kaira are together, right?"

"Yes, that's what our relationship status says on the social networking sites also, isn't it?"

She didn't pay attention to what I said, "Do you know about her past?"

"Yes, I do."

"You even know that she was in an open relationship with her ex even after they were not together?"

I was not able to be in command of my annoyance now; so I stood up and looked at her, "Yes, I know everything. All the information that you have put your effort in collecting and come up with, you could have continued this question and answer meeting over the phone itself."

She looked at me and calmly answered, "Sit down, I requested you not to get frenzied. Listen out, please."

I tagged along with what she said.

"So you know everything about her past with Pratik?"

"I just said yes."

"Are you happy with her?"

"Yes I am, I can only be too bothered about her past. I am her present and she loves me a lot. In fact, I was never so happy before."

"I know Aryan, you are very annoyed with me, esspecially after whatever happened between us that evening. Maybe I over-reacted but have to blame the alcohol partly for the way I reacted with you."

"Forget it, Anushka. The damage has been done and you are getting engaged to someone. So why are you even apologizing? To be very honest, it might sound rude but I cannot forgive you.

Again, I would say, whatever happened has brought out some good results."

"That's your choice, Aryan, and your anger is justified. But are you serious about Kaira?"

"This is my personal life, Anushka and I am not comfortable sharing it with anyone. But to answer your question, yes we are just trying to grow together in every achievable approach and once things click, we will talk to our parents." There was seconds of silence and I continued, "You know what the difference between you and your friend is? I always considered you as my best friend and passionately loved you from my school days, but the end result was you humiliating and lying to me. When it comes to your friend, I barely knew her after you left but she came clean, spoke the truth about her past affairs, clarified and then we started off. Touchwood, things have been good so far."

The type of short tempered girl Anushka is, I was surprised to see her listening to me calmly without interrupting.

Very politely she asked, "What have I lied to you about?"

"You know it better."

"If you are angry because I did not tell you anything about my engagement, then yes it was my fault. I should have at least shared that with you. It is not relevant anymore, I've broken my engagement."

Another unexpected surprise, but this time I controlled myself, "Why?"

"My presence here was more important this time, so I called it off."

"Now what kind of a joke is this? Or is it one of your great revelation attempts?"

"It's not a joke, Aryan. I came to Kolkata for you."

I got up saying, "I am sorry Anushka if you have come for me, I cannot do anything for you here. Moreover, if your silent intention is me, forget it. I can't leave Kaira, not for you. We both have gone through enough from our past and when you left me doomed, this girl stood beside me – No matter what happens, I can't manage to hurt her, so please excuse us this time."

She caught my hand and said, "Sit down and let me finish. After that say whatever you want to."

I again sat down. She asked, "Do you know anyone called Smita?"

I tried to think but was not able to retrieve it from my mind's database. It had shut off for today, "Can't recall anyone by that name."

"She is from the same airline based out in Delhi for training."

I tried thinking again and this time I succeeded. I recollected Kaira's roommates in Delhi, one of them with whom she went out partying on the first day.

I said, "There is a roommate of Kaira in Delhi; her name is Smita. But I don't know her; just heard a few things about her from Kaira."

"Hmm, she is a friend of mine."

"I am confused now."

"Quite natural, now let me explain everything to you." After this, Anushka started off with her explanations "I have a batch mate of mine called Sanghita, we are good friends. Lately, we had started visiting each other's house and I met her sister who was preparing for cabin-crew training. She is Smita, Kaira's roommate."

I did not interrupt, looked at her, indicating 'go ahead'- she continued, "All my batch-mates know about you and many of them advocated to counsel me to say yes to you. Among the old school topics, this same discussion had come up while Smita was still around. We were at Sanghita's place for a girls-night out. Smita got to know a lot about you from her sister.

"While going through old pictures in Orkut, we flipped through a couple of your pictures. When Smita saw your face, her face turned pale". Anushka paused.

"What happened? I am listening, I coanxed her."

Anushka politely said, "I will continue but once again do remember, you promised."

"I will try my best."

"I won't continue then."

"Okay I assure you that I won't get hyper. Now please stop being dramatic and continue"

"When I saw Smita surprised with your photograph, I asked her what the matter was. She said you and her roommate Kaira are seeing each other. I told her everything possible in detail about you, right from your school-time."

I broke my patience, "Indeed! It's a small world we live in today. So what's the point here?"

"Let me finish first."

"Sorry, go ahead."

She continued, "Initially, Smita was uncomfortable talking about her, but later she opened up. The first weekend she went out clubbing with all her new colleagues"

I recollected, yes she is right. Kaira did go out with them and that's the exact same night I tried calling her many times but did not get any response. I was sure by then that a shock was on its way, I so concentrated on what Anushka was saying.

"All of them went out late night and partied hard and your girl who was completely drunk met a guy in that disc. She decided to go to his farm house alone, somewhere isolated in Noida."

I interrupted, "Alone as in?" my voice chocked already.

"Smita and her friends tried convincing her not to go but she did not listen and went off with the stranger. The next day early in the morning, she came back to the guest house. Kaira secretly did confess to Smita as she was close to her that the previous night she had a one night stand with that guy in his farmhouse and also made her swear that she would not reveal this to anyone."

I got furious listening to this, stood up and shouted on Anushka, "I don't believe this. This is a made up story of yours; it's not possible and she can't do this."

Anushka got up and put one of her hands on my shoulder "Aryan, if you don't believe, I am dialing Smita's number. You better talk to her."

I pushed her hand away from my shoulder and walked a little further, "What if your friend is lying?"

"Okay, agreed for a minute that she is lying, but what will she gain out of this?"

Suddenly a flashback swept me away from my feet. Gosh! I did try calling her that night but her cell phone was switched off. I started praying to god that whatever I had heard, should be wrong.

My voice was gone; I had a lump in my throat. The surroundings choked me and I wanted to scream out. I managed to ask, "Is this the reason why you came to Kolkata suddenly?"

"Yes, because I know your kind of temper too well. Before I could tell you everything, you would have disconnected my phone call. When I got to know about your affair, I thought of warning you of her past but a while back I had the impression that she's been telling you everything."

I took out my cell phone from my pocket and started scrolling through the contact list. Anushka came and stood beside me, "What are you doing?"

"I will ask her directly; my heart still says all these allegations are false."

"Go ahead and ask her if that satisfies you, but keep one thing in mind."

"What is it?"

"Smita's name should not come out."

"Hmm." I dialled her number.

Bullets in my heart

"Hi!"

"Hi, dodo!"

"Where are you?"

"I am at the Airport. Why? What happened? You are sounding very different."

"Do you love me?"

"What's wrong, Dodo? Of course I love you."

I was numb, voice badly chocked, desperately trying to stop my tears from bursting out.

She asked again, "Dodo, what happened? Why are you sounding so low?"

"Kaira, I will ask you something. I beg you to kindly tell me the truth."

"What is the problem? Why are you acting so weird?"

"Where were you the night you went out for clubbing for the first time in Delhi?"

"Which night are you talking about?"

Her voice sounded serious now.

"The night I tried calling you and your phone was switched off, kaira. And please don't lie."

"I went out partying with my colleagues to Agnee."

"Where were you after the party?"

"I came back to the guest house."

I was not able to control my temper. I shouted, "For goodness' sake Kaira, why are you lying? You went to a farmhouse outside Delhi with a stranger you met in the Disc." I could literally feel the deep breath I was talking myself.

There was absolute silence over both ends of the line; I tried lowering my voice to a possible extent and asked again. "Please tell me Kaira, is this true? I beg you."

"Who told you this?"

"That's not important."

"Yes Aryan, whoever told you this is true. I went with a stranger. I met at a party."

"And what happened there?"

No response, I asked again in a broken voice, "Answer me."

"Just a one night stand and then he dropped me to the guest house in the morning."

"And after coming back, you called me?"

There was again no response; I continued with tear drops falling and my voice trembling, "Why did you do this? I loved you so much Kaira. I loved you and equally respected you when you told me everything about your past. I was so excited about your new job and was waiting eagerly to meet you." I broke down completely , tears started flowing out heavily, "Why?"

In a helpless tone, Kaira tried to make me feel normal, "Baby, shona, please don't cry. Listen to me! I know what I did was wrong, just got too drunk that day and seriously don't know how it all happened and what made me do that. When I came back the next day, I felt really guilty and even wanted to share this with you but did not have the courage to do so. Dodo, I had the fear of losing you ... Please honey forgive me ... Nothing of this sort will happen ever again."

I somehow was not able to control my tears; people around the place were staring at me. It was embarrassing but there was nothing much to be done; I did not care. Anushka caught both my shoulders tightly from the back to calm me down.

I took a deep breath, "You are free from today, Kaira. I won't bother you again, and you are too sweet. I cannot express how angry I am, how disgusted and broken you're making me."

"Dodo, it was an accident, I am so sorry please baby ... I know it's my fault and I can only be sorry. I will take whatever you give me for this. Nothing ever happened after that, trust me."

"Trust?" I said, "That one night of yours cost me my lifelong trust."

I was quiet, Kaira continued, "My training will be over in a few days. Once I start flying , even if it's just for a day, I will come down to Kolkata to meet you. Honey, I'm sorry it's not only you, even Kaira loves her dodo."

I rubbed my tears and said, "I don't know, I need some sleep. Not feeling well, will talk to you later."

Without even waiting for her response, I disconnected and switched off my cell phone.

Quietly I went back to one of the blocks and sat down completely doomed and shattered. Anushka came and sat beside me.

After effects of truth
"The moment I heard all this, I was not able to stay back and when I recalled what I did to you, I later realized that I should have said *yes* to you long back but I was confused somehow and today I can say I am confident of what I am doing ... I came here for you, Aryan, the same girl you were after since high school. I can't believe, just to make me jealous you hooked up with Kaira.

I knew from beforehand this day would come; she is not your type. So please now cheer up, you have better things to do in your life."

Disregarding whatever she said, I just asked, "You broke your engagement?"

"Yes."

I looked at her and said, "Let's go. I will drop you; go home and take rest."

Looking at her face, I couldn't figure out whether she was shocked or not, but I could tell she somehow tried her level best to not show it.

She answered, "Okay, let's go."

Before dropping her home, I just asked, "When are you leaving for Delhi?"

She replied, "Day after tomorrow."

Without even bidding goodbye, I took a turn and headed home.

It had been three days. I was in no mood to go to the office. Since it was Monday, my great manager gave me some small set of unwanted lectures which I had to digest before getting my sick leave approved. My secret desire then was, if I ever get a good chance in my life, surely I will run my car over him someday.

Faiyaz and gang were less worried about what had happened. I had told him that I would fill him in with everything after I reached work the following day. I then switched my cell phone off to avoid any calls from Kaira or Anushka.

I reminisced everything that had happened after Anushka came and the information she had given me. I was much more normal at home. It's hard to accept but you can't circumvent destiny and I believe the term LOVE is not in my providence. So it's better for me to live single; it might get a little frustrating in the beginning looking at other couples, but when it comes to the long run, I can escape the trouble and humiliation of heartbreaks. Time for taking some serious assessment about my career – no further experiments.

I switched on my laptop and started typing an email.

Hi Anushka,

This email is definitely not to look into your whereabouts or how you are doing. This is about what happened the other day. The ground truth about me that everyone knows is that, with all our innocence and immature heart I have been after you since school days. In spite of numerous fights, destiny placed me in front of you again and again. I can never forgive you but hats off to our friendship, you came all the way back to Kolkata just to stand beside me and help me out in knowing the truth. I am lucky that I have a friend like you; thank you for all your love and affection, though it was never hundred percent mine. If seriously there was anything called love inside of you for me, then this day would have never taken place. We would never be in this situation ever. I will continue to love you, but unlike the way I did before, cheers! The definition of love for you has changed in my dictionary and I cannot think of anything more than our friendship. Yes, right now I would prefer to be loveless. Whatever reason it has been for you to break your engagement and come to me, cannot get much help. You have exhibited your still thriving affection for me, but more than that I will miss the charm of Kaira in my life. She stood beside me when you left me, her sweetness, charm and being realistic towards life gave me a direction in my life and I am confident that I won't be able to feel for you the way I felt for her.

I won't go back to her because for what she has done will always haunt me and the relationship cannot thrive and continue this way. Emotions are dead within me, but yes, I have forgiven her and will always pray to god that whatever she does in her life, she be happy and successful.

You are a terrific girl and I will always regret about our unsuccessful togetherness. I am sure you will get what you are looking for soon in your life.

Now my eyes are wide open from the greatest dream of my existence and it's time for me to concentrate on my career. It's sad and heartbreaking, yet it has to be done because that's what my destiny has in store for me.

Please don't misunderstand me.

With good wishes,

Aryan

So this was my confession, the protagonist Aryan Roy's. I still remember, before writing my final letter to Anushka, for the first time in my life I was sure of what I was doing. More than that, I was completely aware of what I was going to lose. But far beyond that, I am happy today for whatever I have achieved in my life. Nonetheless, the *storm in my mind* is alive, awake and restless (I know it will never die within me).

Epilogue:
One year later

After this confrontation, Aryan realocated from Kolkata to Bangalore for improved career prospects.

The silence between Aryan and Anushka went on for a couple of months; either of the two did not know what to conclude from the situation. They finally got back in touch and Anushka and Aryan are still very good friends. Aryan still offers her love advices about how to find a better guy and both often share good laughs. Aryan is still un-successful in convincing Anushka that his *gyan* sessions will come handy on implementation.

Kaira had contacted Aryan a lot many times, apologized for what she had done many times but it was too late. She was still the wonder girl to him, charming and beautiful as always. Well, fortunately or un-fortunately, she has acquired the very kind of life she dreamed about. Parties, friends, expensive living and living it up across India wherever her flight halted for a layover; everyone can guess where she has sunk in her personal life. He always prays to God for her safety because she was still a child to him and a part of him still cared. They still met time and again; catching up over coffee when she was in Bangalore for layovers, and definitely was whenever there is time for a coffee. She pulled his leg often,

"If I don't get anyone in life, then for sure, I will make you run away with me and marry you."

His maturity never gave in to her joke, since within himself, he would never forgive her. To him she was no longer the kind of girl who could be his wife.

He would joke back, "We are good as friends. How can I even consider marrying you? Have you gone out of your mind?"

She would smile and counter, "Well Mr. Engineer cum writer, my speculation shows that you believe in destiny too much. Let's just see what it finally offers you."